HATTIE EVER AFTER

HATTIE EVER AFTER

Kirby Larson

DELACORTE PRESS

Text copyright © 2013 by Kirby Larson
Jacket art copyright © 2013 by Jonathan Barkat

Photographs on pages 40 and 48 courtesy of the author. Photograph on page 119 courtesy of San Francisco Bay Area Post Card Club, postcard.org.

Visit us on the Web! randomhouse.com/kids
Educators and librarians, for a variety of teaching tools, visit us at
RHTeachersLibrarians.com

Library of Congress Cataloging-in-Publication Data
Larson, Kirby.
Hattie ever after / Kirby Larson. — 1st ed.
p. cm.
Sequel to: Hattie Big Sky.
Summary: In 1919, seventeen-year-old Hattie leaves the Montana prairie—and her sweetheart Charlie—to become a female reporter in San Francisco.
ISBN 978-0-385-73746-3 (hc) — ISBN 978-0-307-97968-1 (ebk) —
ISBN 978-0-385-90668-5 (glb)
[1. Self-reliance—Fiction. 2. Orphans—Fiction. 3. Reporters and reporting—Fiction. 4. San Francisco (Calif.)—History—20th century—Fiction.] I. Title.
PZ7.L32394Hb 2013   [Fic]—dc23   2012007068

The text of this book is set in 12-point Adobe Garamond.
Book design by Vikki Sheatsley

Printed in the United States of America
10 9 8 7 6 5 4 3 2 1
First Edition

For everyone who asked what was next for Hattie,
with affection and appreciation

❧ 1 ❧

Homesteads and Hamlet Traps

June 4, 1919
Great Falls, Montana
Brown's Boardinghouse

Dear Perilee,

*You will never guess what I am posting in the mail
besides this letter to you: my last check to Mr. Nefzger!
After these long months, Uncle Chester's IOU is paid in
full. When first presented with that IOU some months
ago, I couldn't imagine how on earth I would repay
it. Especially after that summer hailstorm knocked
down my crops along with my hopes of making a go of
the farm. The good Lord has quite a sense of humor,
plunking me down here in Great Falls, in just the sort*

1

of job I left Iowa to escape, though I must confess, it was pure pleasure this past winter to have indoor plumbing. No more walking to the necessary when it's forty below! And I've certainly perfected essential cleaning skills. I'll have you know that I can now make a bed, scour the washbowl, and Hoover-sweep the carpet in a lodger's room in fifteen minutes flat.

Despite the glamour of my current position, I am counting the minutes until the next thing. What is that, you ask? I do not know. You are right, as always, that the sensible plan is to come to you in Seattle. Of course, I would love to be neighbors again, as we were on the Montana prairie. But you know I am not prone to the sensible. What sensible girl would have said yes to spending a year under Montana's big sky, trying to make a go of a long-lost uncle's homestead claim?

And what sensible girl wouldn't say yes to Charlie, who is quite convinced we are meant to grow old together? Only a fool would deflect his attentions. Well, I saw such a fool in the mirror this morning.

It's not that Charlie wouldn't be easy to look at for the next fifty years. Aside from your Karl, I can't think of another man so solid, kind, and true-blue. What is it that I want, one may wonder, if not to be Mrs. Charlie Hawley? That's as much a mystery to me as Uncle Chester's past. But I feel strongly that Hattie Here-and-There must change her life before she can change her name.

I still puzzle over Uncle Chester, God rest his soul,

calling himself a scoundrel. Perhaps this world needs
more such scoundrels. Without him, I never would
have had the chance to test myself on the homestead, to
breathe in the promises carried on a prairie breeze, or to
fill my heart with so many friends, among whom I count
you the dearest.

    Mrs. Brown is hollering for me. She is in a perfect
dither over the acting troupe soon to arrive. The
Venturing Varietals are sure to be livelier boarders than
our usual Fuller Brush salesmen.

Your friend,
Hattie Inez Brooks

The floor began to vibrate beneath my feet. Mrs. Brown had progressed from hollering to pounding the ceiling below with the broom handle. Evidently, the workday had begun. I set the letter to Perilee aside, tied my apron on, and went to find my employer.

She was in the kitchen, kneading bread dough. I was not to be trusted with this particular task. Despite Perilee's expert tutelage, I never managed to bake a loaf of bread any lighter than a flatiron.

Mrs. Brown clapped floury hands together. "Busy now! I want things spotless when the actors arrive. Spotless!" She slapped the dough for emphasis.

Taking stock of what yet needed to be done, I dragged a rug outside, threw it across the clothesline, and began to beat it clean.

As I swung the rug-beater back and forth, my thoughts

back-and-forthed, too, settling first on a snippet from Charlie's last letter:

I should be grateful to be home. And I am, don't mistake me. Too many families lost their sons in that war. It's hard to explain what I feel. The best I can come up with is that it's like trying to pitch without a baseball. Something's missing. And I think you know what that something is.

I shook my head. Why couldn't I be more like other girls my age? Take Mrs. Brown's niece. She spent her every waking hour sizing up this beau or that, stitching tea towels and petticoats and putting aside a little each month for a set of Spode Buttercup dishes.

Perhaps I'd have been the same way had it not been for Uncle Chester leaving me the homestead in his will. Last year, working to prove up, I had been more than Hattie Here-and-There, the orphan girl with too many temporary homes. I had been Hattie Big Sky, carving out a place to belong. Like so many others who'd been drawn to Montana's prairie, I was not successful. And losing the farm was not the worst of my losses. It was nothing compared to losing Mattie.

I stopped my exertions and swiped at my eyes, suddenly thankful for this dusty job. Should anyone come upon me, I could blame *it* for my damp eyes, not memories of Mattie. The influenza had cut a wide swath of death through this country, but that one loss cut an even wider swath through my heart.

After a moment, I resumed the rhythmic slapping of beater on rug, another thought moving to the forefront of my mind. For all its challenges and sorrows, my time on the homestead had given me a taste of what it might be like to stake out my own claim on life, and had left me craving more.

After a while, I carted the last rug into the house, smoothing it back in its place on the floor. Windows were next. I lugged buckets and rags upstairs, catching my reflection in the glass in the Daisy room. Guilt was stamped all over my face. For good reason: I had been less than forthcoming with Perilee, my truest friend, in my letter to her. I *did* know what I wanted to do. Six long lonely months here in Great Falls had provided ample time to piece together new hopes.

Those Honyocker's Homilies I'd written from the homestead for the *Arlington News* back in Iowa were the first fleas to bite. Then I began to read the assorted newspapers our lodgers left behind, discovering articles written by female reporters like muckraker Ida Tarbell. And Nellie Bly, who earned her first assignment at eighteen, just a year older than me.

I could not yet confess it to anyone, not even Perilee, but I had thrown a lasso around a dream even bigger than a Montana farm.

I wanted to be a reporter.

Even though I was about as worldly as Rooster Jim's hens, I did know that a mild talent and a few pieces published in a small-town paper were not sufficient. Women like Nellie Bly did Grand Things; that was how they got to be real writers. Despite its name, Great Falls was hardly the place to do something grand.

Neither was Arlington, Iowa. And even though my heart approved of Charlie's plan for an "us," my mind feared that saying yes to him was saying no to myself. I needed to find my own place in the world. My own true place.

And something in me believed *that* place was connected to the working end of a pen, not a plow. And certainly not a polishing cloth! Every night, after I was done for the day at Mrs. Brown's, I'd been scribbling away in children's composition books—the cheapest I could find at the five-and-dime. I copied down inspiring words and snippets of poems, but mostly I used those pages to practice being a reporter.

The first article in my book was about Mrs. Brown's neighbor Sam Blessing, who had the brains of a chicken. No, that was an insult to chickens. In a fit of pique at his wife, Sam had shut himself in the shed out back. The shed that locked from the outside. Equally piqued, his wife had not been inclined to unlock the door. It took some serious horse trading on his part to coax her to wield the key and let him out. The bargain they'd struck was reflected in the headline I'd written: "Mrs. Sam Blessing's Mother to Visit Great Falls for Three Months."

I was also partial to the piece I'd written about Mrs. Maynard's dog, Blue. Mrs. Maynard would send Blue, by himself, to the grocer's with her shopping list and market basket, and he would return with the requested provisions, carrying the basket handle in his mouth. "Course, I don't send him after cream," she'd told me, "lest it would be butter by the time he trotted it home."

I'd written about the children's story times at the public

library and the Sons of Norway parade, and had even tried my hand at writing a review of the last movie I'd seen at the Gem.

It was all in secret. Not a soul knew about my efforts. Had I tried, I might have been able to get one or two of my stories published in the *Great Falls Tribune*.

I paused in midscrub of a window, vinegar water dripping down my arm. *Might have.* But shopping dogs and stubborn men are hardly topics to occupy a real reporter's time.

My thoughts were interrupted by voices below. Many voices. Melodious voices. The Varietals had arrived!

I finished the window, ditched bucket and rags, and hurried downstairs. Several people, bearing an inordinate amount of luggage, were crowded into the front hall. A young dandy with Brylcreemed hair struck a pose by the coat tree. An ingénue with pouty lips fussed with the hem of her jacket. An older actress wore an overcoat of midnight-blue wool that tapered to an impossibly thin waist before ending a fashionable four inches above her shoe tops. She caught me gawking and I was rewarded with a queenly nod.

Their leader, Mr. Lancaster, stroked his waxed goatee as he parleyed terms with Mrs. Brown. "We have a train to catch on Saturday," he said.

"Only three nights?" Mrs. Brown's voice registered disappointment.

"Regrettably, that is the case." Mr. Lancaster bowed to Mrs. Brown, reached for her hand, and planted a kiss there. "Such is the life of the wandering performer. Now, would you be so kind as to show us to our rooms?"

I headed to the kitchen to start noon dinner as Mrs. Brown settled everyone to rights. The door soon swung open and the Brylcreem man popped his head in. "Might I trouble you for directions to a tobacconist's?" His smile was straight from an advertisement for Pepsodent toothpaste, it was that white. "I myself do not indulge. But Miss Clare is convinced that Milo cigarettes help relax her vocal cords."

I gave him directions; for which my reward was another glittering smile.

He had barely exited the room when one of the young women of the troupe slipped in.

"Tobacconist's?" I asked, anticipating her question.

"What?" She looked puzzled.

"Sorry. That young man with the white smile was just here, asking for directions. I assumed you might need them, too."

"Cecil?" Her cheeks flushed pink. "I mean, Mr. Hall?"

I started in on a stack of spuds that needed peeling. "I hope I didn't sound rude. Can I help you?"

"I noticed the clothesline out back. Might I hang some of the costumes for tonight's performance out to air? You can't imagine how"—she waggled her eyebrows—"aromatic they get with all those wearings."

"The neighbors will appreciate the change of scenery," I said. "Much more interesting than Mrs. Brown's bloomers."

She laughed. "I can imagine."

I showed her to the bucket of clothespins and she went after the costumes, hanging them out to air.

"Oh, you're making scalloped potatoes," she said, passing back through the kitchen when she'd finished. "My favorite."

I took stock of her. There was none of the oiliness that I'd felt from Mr. Hall. And she looked to be about my age. I introduced myself. "Would you like a cup of coffee?"

"Oh, I'd love one." She sat at the table. "I'm Sylvia. The world's worst wardrobe mistress, according to her nibs in there." She took the coffee I offered but shook her head at sugar and cream.

"I thought this job would be so exciting." Sylvia rolled her eyes. " 'Wardrobe mistress' is only a fancy term for chief laundress and mender. And all the travel. After this, we're off to San Francisco." Elbows on the table, she rested her chin on her hands, wearing a decidedly glum expression.

Imagine feeling blue about going somewhere like San Francisco. Think of the doings in such a place! A person could write news stories there till her arm fell off. "Why do you keep with it?" I asked, sprinkling flour over the top of the potatoes in the baking dish.

She glanced around, then ducked her head close to mine. "Cecil," she whispered.

I wrinkled my forehead, trying to think. *See sill?* What? Then it hit me. "You mean Mr. Hall?"

Sylvia put her finger to her lips. "Our secret, promise?"

"Cross my heart."

"You're a peach." She gave me a friendly wink. "The coffee hit the spot. Thanks. Back to the salt mines."

She paused with her hand on the swinging door. "Say. Would you like to come to the show tomorrow night? I can get you a ticket. On the house."

A live vaudeville show. I'd never seen one before. And for free! "That's kind of you. I'd love it."

9

"It will be quite the performance." She flashed a mysterious smile. "One you won't want to miss."

Thanks to Sylvia's generosity, the next night I found myself in a plush maroon seat in the tenth row, center section, of the Grand Opera House. I held the printed program in gloved hands. Out of loyalty to my benefactor, the first thing I did was look for Cecil Hall's name. There it was, in minuscule print, near the bottom of the last page. Taking up most of the program were the names of Ellington Lancaster—"Founder and Principal, Venturing Varietals" and "Marquis of the Footlights"—and Vera Clare, who was not only "Empress of Emotion" but also "Queen of the Varietal Stage."

My neighbor was a chatty woman whose hat would've been better suited to someone with a face less like a pumpkin. She pointed to Cecil's name on the program. "I saw him in Helena," she confided. "He plays a magician that makes himself disappear." Her eyes twinkled. "My nephew told me how it's done. It's called a Hamlet trap. They rig up this door in the stage floor. The actor steps on it just so and *poof!* Gone." She sighed. "I come all this way to see him again."

The burgundy velvet curtain began to rise, earning me a poke in the ribs from my neighbor. For a plump woman, she had sharp bones. "Show's starting," she stage-whispered.

I nodded, edging myself a bit farther away from that pain-inflicting elbow as I settled in to enjoy the evening. The opening act was a comic duo from Great Falls. They performed a skit involving an accordion, a ridiculously large woman's hat, and a wheelbarrow. I laughed so hard, I thought I might slip right out of my chair and into the aisle.

Vera Clare was stunning in her role as a grieving mother in a short play called *Mama's Boys*. I wept as hard as I'd laughed earlier. For a small woman, she radiated great stage presence. All around me, audience members—even men!—were dabbing eyes with handkerchiefs. To think that Sylvia found traveling with such a troupe to be wearing! From my plush seat, the dramatic life seemed nothing but thrilling.

After the intermission, Cecil's time in the spotlight finally arrived. I had to admit, he did look dashing in that black top hat and red-satin-lined magician's cape. I found his delivery a trifle melodramatic, but my neighbor could not take her eyes from him up there in the footlights. She grabbed my arm as he moved center stage. "The line will be 'Exemptum exactum,'" she murmured. No sooner had she uttered the words than Cecil, too, pronounced them, though much more theatrically.

"Exemptum exactum!" His baritone voice rang out over the hall. Then, with a swoosh of his cape, he vanished. A woman behind me shrieked in surprise. My heart raced and I gripped the seat arms. Even though I'd been forewarned, Cecil's departure was exceedingly dramatic.

It wasn't until later that I would learn exactly *how* dramatic it had been.

❧ 2 ❧

Hattie Stay or Hattie Go

June 6, 1919

Dear Perilee,

*Who would have imagined I would have news to
write of, and so soon after my last letter. I attended the
Venturing Varietals' performance last night, which ended
up being doubly theatrical! They are good, very good,
especially that Miss Vera Clare, but she was upstaged by
a vanishing act—one of the male actors eloped with the
wardrobe mistress, Sylvia, and they went back to her
family in Minneapolis. She was very sweet. I would've
thought she could do better, but what I know about men
and women would fit on a postage stamp.*

There are dramatic gestures and woe-is-mes galore,

but you can bet, despite all the to-do, the actors will still want their breakfast on time. I best get at it.

Hattie

I switched on the kitchen light and was startled to find that someone had been sitting in the dark. It was Miss Vera Clare, all afroth in a filmy lavender dressing gown. Her face, cleansed of makeup, was weary and lined. No one would mistake her for a rare beauty of the stage at this moment.

"I couldn't sleep," she said. "So I started the coffee."

I got out mugs, sugar, and cream. The percolator gave a dainty *blurp* to signal it was done brewing. Miss Clare stirred four heaping teaspoons of sugar into the filled mug I handed her.

"You've heard the news, I would imagine." She took a tentative sip, then stirred in another spoonful.

I nodded and began beating eggs in a bowl.

"Evidently, they'd been planning this since we played Chicago." She closed her eyes, leaning her head against the chair back, and patted at the underside of her chin with the back of her left hand. After a dozen or so pats, she righted her head. "I recommend this exercise. With your round face, you'll be prone to creping in the neck. Most unbecoming."

I'd never given my neck much thought before, aside from the occasional wince when I got a crick in it. At Miss Clare's words, however, I felt its flesh begin to loosen and wrinkle. I lifted my head a bit higher.

She fussed with the bow on her dressing gown. "Thank heavens, that's not my worry."

"A crepey neck?" I wasn't following.

"No. No." The look she gave me would've curdled milk. "A troupe of our stature simply cannot perform without a wardrobe mistress. It isn't done. Would Sarah Bernhardt have been expected to perform without attendants?"

Her question was being asked of the air, not me. I poured the eggs in the skillet, stirring so they didn't burn.

"Surely you can see our dilemma?"

I surely wished she could see mine! I had to finish preparing breakfast, and she was driving me to distraction with her conversation. "Surely," I said, hoping her rant had run its course and she'd remove herself to her room to dress—on her own, without an attendant—for the breakfast that I would be expected to serve—on my own, without an attendant—in very short order.

"I thought so. Hazel eyes are the sign of a sharp intellect." She finished her coffee, setting the cup on the table as she rose to her feet. "We would require a firm commitment until we reach San Francisco, where we will no doubt be able to find someone more qualified. The pay is adequate and your lodgings would be covered."

I pulled a warmed serving dish from the oven and piled it full of eggs, scrambled to the color of yellow jonquils. It was as I stepped away from the stove toward the door to the dining room that Miss Clare's words hit me. "Are you offering me a job?"

She pulled her dressing gown snug around her. "We need a wardrobe mistress, and you seem the likeliest choice in this one-horse town."

I bobbled the serving bowl. Was I hearing correctly?

14

"We leave tomorrow. And you would need to leave with us."

Like a tiny violet tornado, Miss Vera Clare spun from the room and up the back stairs, leaving me to consider her offer. Well, not so much an offer as a command. Did she even know my name?

My mind awhirl with her proposition, I twice refilled Mr. Lancaster's teacup with coffee as I served breakfast. I was thankful when the meal ended and I could finally retire to the kitchen to stand in front of a sink full of suds. That was the best spot for thinking, I'd learned.

As I scrubbed, two voices whispered around me. Hattie Go spoke into my right ear: "Don't you see? This is your chance to do something Grand."

Hattie Stay buzzed in my left ear. "What about Charlie? What will he think if you move even farther away?"

"He'd want you to have that adventure," urged Hattie Go. "Want you to pursue your dreams."

"He wants you to marry him!" protested Hattie Stay.

"The Pacific Ocean!" sighed Hattie Go. "Think of it!"

I could almost smell salty air. Hear clanging cable cars. See Nob Hill. And fog. I'd only read about such things, in one of the books Uncle Chester had left behind. Sights and sounds and smells that would nourish my seedling writer's dreams like water and sun.

I shook out the dish towel, trying to shake out the voices bickering in my head.

"Oh, Hattie." Mrs. Brown stepped through the swinging door. "Here are my ideas for dinner today."

I took them from her. "This looks pretty fancy." I glanced

at the clock. How would I get everything accomplished in time for dinner at noon?

"My thoughts exactly." She smiled. "I'm counting on Mr. Lancaster to spread the word about us to other troupes."

I held up the menu. "In that case, are you sure you want *me* to bake the cake?"

"If you sift the flour twice, it should be fine. Now, I'm going to tidy up the parlor and answer some mail before my Ladies' Aid meeting. If I'm not there to stop them, they'll put Millie Sewell in charge of the Flag Day picnic." She shuddered. "I'll be back in time to help set the table." She pushed out the swinging door, then pivoted right back in.

"Oh, this came for you yesterday. I forgot about it, what with all the hubbub." She tossed an envelope at me as she left the room. I caught it and saw that it was from Leafie. This was only the second letter she'd sent, so I tore it open right then and there.

Dear Hattie,

Excuse the wobbly handwriting, but your tomcat is making a nuisance of himself. Seems he feels it's time for his afternoon snack of sardines and cream. Turns out if you give a cat a treat once, he expects it every day! I wouldn't mind except he's growing so stout he nearly knocked me out of my own bed last night.

Rooster Jim sure enjoyed the last note you sent him. Carries it everywhere! Your letters make us feel like we're right there in Great Falls. You do have a way with words.

Now, I hope you are sitting for this news: Traft Martin carted your old claim shack over to the schoolhouse, where it is now the home of the Vida, Montana, Lending Library. So much for old dogs not being able to learn new tricks! Wouldn't Chester get a kick out of that, him being such a bookworm?

I did not read the enclosed. Figured it was none of my business. But of course I won't hardly sleep until I know what's inside. Quite a shock getting a letter for Chester. Following so close on Traft's actions, I nearly had to take to my bed to recover.

My nose will twitch with curiosity until I hear from you.

All best,
Leafie

I peered inside the envelope postmarked "Vida" and slid out another, smaller envelope, this one from San Francisco. Imagine the coincidence! I opened it, and as I pulled out the letter it held, something small fell into my apron pocket. I left it and took up the letter.

Dearest Chester,

We agreed long ago that you would come should I ever send the enclosed. I hope with all my heart that you will return it in person, as I care more to see the bearer than the token itself.

Yours,
Ruby

That was all it said. I looked for more clues on the envelope. Aside from the postmarked date—April 11—there was only the return address and, above that, "R. Danvers." I reached into my apron pocket and fished out the dropped object.

I had seen such a thing before, when I'd lived in Kentucky with that one set of cousins. The eldest—what was her name?—had come home all aglow one night, bearing a similar token. The one now in my hand had started life as a Mercury dime. Mercury's image had been filed away from the face of the coin and replaced with two sets of initials, carved with careful elegance: *C.W.* and *R.D.* With my thumb, I traced the froth of lacy engraving skimming the edges of those four precious letters.

Chester Wright. Ruby Danvers.

When that Kentucky cousin had been gifted her engraved token, she proclaimed it signified true love. In this case, I couldn't say what the token meant. I knew very little about Uncle Chester, despite his bequeathing me his homestead claim, though in his one and only letter to me, he'd called himself a scoundrel. Other than that, he was a cipher.

Now another question mark: Ruby Danvers. Was she Uncle Chester's lost love? The one whose traces I'd found in the trunk he'd left behind? My crystal ball was as clear as if it'd been filled with Montana gumbo mud.

C.W. and *R.D.* I pressed the token into my palm. Here was yet one more mystery about my scoundrel uncle.

A mystery that, thanks to Mr. Cecil Hall, I now had a chance of solving.

The coin grew warm in my hand. My last check to Mr. Nefzger had been mailed off. If I went to San Francisco, I could always go on to Seattle—or back to Arlington—afterward.

I untied my apron and hung it up slowly.

Eyes squeezed tight, I said a prayer. "Lord, you have moved in many mysterious ways in my short life. If I am supposed to go, I'd sure appreciate a sign." Slowly, I opened my eyes, taking in every inch of the kitchen for the answer to my prayer.

Nothing inside the room had changed. I glanced out the window. No miraculous rainbow or bolt of lightning. I was on my own here.

I placed my right palm on the swinging kitchen door, standing half in, half out. At that moment, a memory overtook me. I'd been held after school, as Miss Simpson was determined to improve my penmanship by requiring me to copy a sentence on the chalkboard. Fifty times I'd written, "Of all the words of tongue or pen, the saddest are these: it might have been."

There was my lightning bolt. Else why had that particular memory come unbidden? I smoothed my hair and marched into the parlor to give Miss Clare my answer.

I caught Mrs. Brown in the vestibule on her way out and told her of my decision, too. Upon receiving the news, she looked positively distressed. I think it had less to do with me and more to do with the spot she was in. I assured her I'd fix the midday dinner but told her I would need the evening to prepare.

"That's decent of you, Hattie," my almost-former employer told me. "Let's hope Mrs. Whitcomb's at the meeting today. Her cousin might make a suitable replacement."

I put the letter and the coin in my skirt pocket and then transformed myself into a veritable conjurer of cookery, measuring flour here, separating eggs there, and stirring, stirring, stirring all the while. With various pots bubbling away, I patted dry the chicken pieces, then dipped them in buttermilk. When I slid the first drumstick into the pan, hot oil splashed out, stinging my cheek and staining my second-best shirtwaist. One more thing to do before packing! I snatched a rag to wipe off the oil, dragging it through the buttermilk, which ran down my arm and onto my skirt. I grabbed another rag to clean my skirt and knocked over the mixing bowl filled with flour measured out for the biscuits. In a few short minutes, the kitchen was a shambles and I looked like a chicken leg, dipped in buttermilk and flour and fit to fry.

At that very moment someone rapped at the back door. "Oh, go away, will you!" I snapped. But the knocking continued. Frazzled senseless, I threw open the door, ready to give whoever stood there a large piece of my mind.

"Do you really want me to go away?" Charlie asked. "I just got here."

❧ 3 ❧

Burnt Biscuits and Beaus

A kiss can be a comma, a question mark or an exclamation point. —*Mistinguett, French actress*

"Charlie!" I screamed, and threw my arms around his neck, scratching my cheek on his starched collar as I hugged him close, breathing in his good Charlie smell of peppermint and pine soap. Then I pushed back to take him all in, head to toe. It'd been two long years since I'd seen him off at the train station, years that had brought some changes our correspondence hadn't revealed. Those changes added up to more than a few inches in height. He'd gone off a boy of seventeen and returned a man. There was a new scar across his left eyebrow and an unfamiliar expression—sorrow? worry? I wasn't sure—across that familiar face. But other than that, he was

Charlie, through and through. And home safe from that terrible war.

I pressed my hand to my chest, trying to ease the sudden pain there at the thought of all the boys who didn't make it back. Seeing him here, his good self right in front of me, completely unexpected, knowing I'd just made a decision that might break his heart, I did the only prudent thing a person could do. I burst into tears.

Charlie dropped his bag and scooped me close. "What's all this?"

I indulged in a several-minute deluge, making a complete muddle of the both of us. Finally, I gathered myself together and pushed away. "I've made you a horrible mess." Cried out, I dried my face with my apron.

"You can make a mess of me any time." He smiled again. In an instant, I was taken back to the day we'd met, when he'd walked me home from Arlington High School after I'd come to stay at Uncle Holt and Aunt Ivy's. I'd been so shy, I couldn't even get my own name out. But that didn't bother him. He'd talked enough for the both of us. It was him, too, who'd given me Mr. Whiskers, that sassy old tomcat. I don't know how Charlie knew that that bundle of fur and purr was just what a lonely orphan girl needed, but he did.

He took in the boiling pots, the biscuit fixings, and the sizzling skillet on the stove. "It looks like my timing is bad."

Oh, if he only knew. I opened my mouth to tell him of my plans, but the words got stuck somewhere between my head and my heart.

"Shall I come back later?"

Later? There was very little later left. "Charlie . . . well, I . . . There's something—" I had hoped to deliver my news via letter, not in person. "I had no idea you were coming."

He grinned. "That's not the only big surprise. Can you sneak away for a walk?"

I gestured at the pots and pans. "Not till after dinner."

"Looks like you could use a hand."

"Or two!" I picked up a towel and began cleaning up the mess.

Charlie snapped off a salute. "Private Hawley reporting for duty!"

I shook my head. "You? Cook?"

"You'd be surprised at all the army taught me. About airplane engines *and* how to make my way around a kitchen."

"*That* I would like to see!" I finished sweeping up the last of the spilled flour.

"All right, then." He grabbed a spare apron, tying it around his middle. He looked so ridiculous, I couldn't help laughing.

"Laugh all you want," he said with a very serious face. "But you'll have crow to eat for your supper after you taste my biscuits."

He wore the Charlie look I knew so well. The set of the chin and fixed gaze that said, "I can do this; try and tell me I can't." It was the same look he'd worn when Del Bradford had said no one could climb to the tiptop of the old cottonwood tree by the schoolhouse. Or when the other boys on the baseball team said it was impossible to teach a girl—me!—to pitch. Or when he'd been told he was too young to enlist in the fight against the Kaiser. Tree climbed, girl taught, enlisted and served. Check, check, check. Sometimes it seemed to me that Charlie saw life's challenges as a mere list of items to tick off, one after another. If he had set his mind to cooking, it would be a safe bet to say he could cook circles around me. Leastways, I wasn't in the position to turn down an offer of help right then. "Here's the plan. I'll handle the salad and chicken and you can tackle the biscuits and cake."

As I fried and sliced and simmered, I knew I should tell Charlie about San Francisco. Should have told him the very second he arrived. But opportunity doesn't nibble twice at the same hook. My news was like a heavy stone in a muddy pond, sinking deeper and deeper into my gut.

Cross my heart. I would tell him right after the meal. No matter what.

When the troupe and Mrs. Brown—and Charlie—sat down to dinner at noon, compliments flowed faster than water over the Great Falls. "This chicken is so crisp," said Mr. Lancaster. "The biscuits are like biting into clouds," said the ventriloquist. "I shouldn't," said Miss Clare, patting her tiny waist. "But that cake is so delicious, I will have seconds." Had I baked the cake, rather than Charlie, she would not have made such a request. Her comment earned me a Charlie wink, accompanied by a wicked smile, but he never revealed his role as kitchen elf.

Even though he was my friend, I was not allowed to sit and eat. Mrs. Brown was particular about holding the line between staff and guests. Being that I *was* still help, I made sure I did indeed *help*, hovering around the groaning dining room table throughout the entire meal.

Charlie had finished recounting the most entertaining story about a battlefield baseball game using gas masks as mitts. While everyone enjoyed the laugh, I hurried back into the kitchen to refill the coffee carafe. Task accomplished, I pushed open the door and returned to the dining room as Mr. Lancaster reached over and slapped Charlie on the back. "I'm sure you got your share of Huns over there. Showed them a thing or two," he said, making a motion in the air as if jabbing with a bayonet.

Charlie's face gave nothing away, but I noticed his knuckles whitening on the handle of his coffee cup.

"Would you like a refill?" I stood to Mr. Lancaster's left, coffeepot poised to pour.

"Have you served in uniform, sir?" Charlie's voice was level. Too level.

I tried to catch his eye. He only wrinkled his brow in acknowledgment of my glance.

"No. No." Mr. Lancaster cleared his throat. "A minor health defect," he said, waving his hand vaguely.

"It is nothing to joke about." Charlie folded his napkin oh-so-carefully and with equal care set it on the table. I moved around, refilling cups quickly, until I was at his side. On his side. He continued. "Not one day goes by that I don't think about those who did not come home to meals like this. No matter which side they fought on." He pushed his chair back so abruptly that I had to hop to get out of the way. "Thank you for your hospitality, Mrs. Brown. I should be going." He nodded a farewell to the others. "Hattie, may I carry anything into the kitchen for you?"

I couldn't trust my voice. I merely shook my head. Though I had yet to finish offering refills, I followed Charlie back through the swinging door.

In all the years I'd known him, I'd never seen him angry. Never. My hands were trembling so, I had to set the coffee carafe down before I dropped it.

"I didn't mean to ruin our visit by losing my temper," he said.

"Don't." I held up my hand to stop him. "He was thoughtless."

He brushed back a lock of hair that had fallen over his forehead. "Men like that—who think they understand war when they haven't fought—well, I just want to knock some sense into them." He held up a fist; then a rueful look came over his face. "That doesn't add up, does it?"

I put both hands over his clenched one. "I'm on *your* side," I said. "Besides, the last time we sparred, I walloped you, remember?"

His face relaxed into a smile. "You had quite the advantage in that I would never hit a girl." He bent over and rubbed his shin. "I still carry the mark of that sharp kick you gave me." He tugged on his pant leg as if to show me the scar. That lightened the mood.

"You deserved it for saying I smelled like a monkey." I started to fill the sink with suds.

He put his arm on mine. "Can that wait a bit?"

I hesitated. I'd told Mrs. Brown I would cook and serve

this last meal, but hadn't made any promises about cleaning up. "How about that walk now?" I suggested. A short walk would still leave me time to pack my things for the trip. For *tomorrow's* trip.

I grabbed my hat and a shawl. Charlie offered his arm and we stepped outside. He leaned in a bit and made a production of sniffing the air. "You know, you don't smell much like a monkey anymore."

That remark earned him an elbow jab.

"And you clean up real nice, too." He squeezed my arm with his. "It's so good to see you."

I squeezed back. "You too." I meant the words. It *was* good to see him healthy and whole. But I'd forgotten about his eyes. They pulled me to him like a magnet. There were lines around them now, since the war, which only served to make him more handsome.

A gust came up, tugging on my hat. "Oh!" I grabbed for it but it sailed a few feet away. Charlie ran after it, brushed it off, then brought it back to me.

"May I have the honor?" He held the hat over my head.

I nodded and he settled it on top of my windblown hair. "I must have lost the hat pin."

As he snugged it on my head, his fingers brushed my cheek, loosening the strings in my legs. I teetered and he caught me.

"Are you all right?" He peered into my face with those eyes.

I nodded again, looking away. It was a lie, of course. I wasn't all right. How could I have been so certain a few hours ago that I'd made the right choice in taking the job with the

Varietals? It was much easier to leave the thought of Charlie than to leave the real—and unfairly attractive—thing. What had I done? What was I doing?

My thoughts were razor-edged and painful against my temples. I would have to ask Mrs. Brown for some of her headache powder when I got back. This whole business between men and women made me feel as cantankerous as my old cow, Violet. Had I four hooves, I'd be stamping them; a tail, and I would be twitching it back and forth in a frenzy. If only Perilee weren't so far away. She'd helped me learn to quilt and bake; surely she could help me with lessons of the heart.

But she wasn't here, and I had to confess to Charlie what I'd done. It was only fair, especially after he'd come all this way. Wait—why *had* he come all this way? He had yet to tell me. But I knew him well enough to know his motives would be revealed on his own timetable.

"This is nice," Charlie said when we reached the park at the end of Central Avenue. While we strolled around the pond in the center of the lawn, he caught me up on the doings back in Arlington. "Did you hear that Miss Simpson is getting married?"

"No." I'd thought our English teacher would be an old maid forever. "Really?"

He nodded. "You'll never guess the lucky groom."

I wracked my brain for possibilities. "I can't imagine."

"Mr. Miltenberger!"

"The newspaper editor?" I grinned. "Why, it's the perfect match. She can correct all of his misspellings!"

"The Ladies' Aid Society is quite relieved that at least one of their matchmaking efforts has succeeded." Charlie bent to pick up a rock and tossed it in the pond.

My stomach flip-flopped. It was time to tell him. Now. "Charlie—" I pressed my hand to my cheek.

"Yes?" He turned to look at me.

Resist the eyes! "There's something, I mean, I want to—"

"You're wondering why I surprised you like this?"

I am a coward. Lily-livered through and through. Charlie had tossed me a lifeline and I grabbed it. "Yes. Yes. That's it."

"I wanted to tell you in person." He reached out and grabbed my hands. "My sergeant's from Seattle, which is where the Boeing company is. I think I wrote you about them before. Still small but Sarge thinks they're up-and-comers."

"So you're going out to interview?"

Charlie cocked his head and looked at me. With those eyes. "That's the good news part." He jabbed both thumbs at his chest. "You are looking at an oh-ficial employee of the Boeing Airplane Company!"

"A job? In Seattle?"

He chuckled. "You should have heard Mother! Here she thought she'd got me home to stay." His face grew serious. "But I couldn't, Hattie. I would've dried up like wheat in a drought."

I hesitated. "I understand your mother's feelings, though. Seattle's a long ways away."

He turned his eyes, his secret weapons, on me again. "Yes, but that's where your friends Karl and Perilee are, and their family. And I thought that's where you wanted to be."

I couldn't move. Couldn't breathe.

"Isn't that right?"

"Charlie—"

"I know I haven't given you much time to think. Springing it on you this way. You'll have packing up to do here, that sort of thing."

"Stop." I put my hands over my ears. "Please stop."

His face was a question mark. "I thought you'd be happy."

I drew in a deep breath, gathering my thoughts. "If the Boeing company has the job you want, I am happy. For you. And you're right. I would love nothing more than to be close to Perilee again."

"And what about being close to me?"

I put my finger to my lips to signal that he should stop talking. "Aunt Ivy always drove me batty, quoting Scripture when she wanted me to do something I didn't want to do. But I keep thinking of those verses from Ecclesiastes—'To everything there is a season. . . .'" Now tears stung at my eyes. I could scarcely believe I was going to say these words and yet I knew I must. "I think this is my season for something else." I couldn't go on.

His eyes darkened with pain. "Have you met someone?"

"No. No! I should have told you right off. I have a new job, too." I couldn't face his gaze. "Charlie, you are so dear to me. But like the war changed you, the homestead changed me. I know there is something I must do before, before I—" I couldn't say the word "marry." "Before I settle down."

"And so?" He stiffened, stepped away from me.

"I'm going to San Francisco. With the Varietals." I touched

my mother's watch, pinned to my bodice. As if it might give me strength to somehow survive the next few moments. "Tomorrow."

It felt as if a boulder had been rolled between us, one we could neither see around nor over. Certainly not through.

When he spoke, it was to say, "I should probably get you back."

We walked in silence as we returned to Brown's. At the door, though, he took me by the arms, turning me to face him full-on.

"Hattie, what is it that you're looking for?" He ducked his head to meet my eyes with his.

I managed a trembling smile. "That's the trouble. I don't know. I only know that I haven't found it yet."

He stared at me for the longest time, then rubbed his hands along my arms. "Well, in that case, you'd best keep looking." His voice was low and each word was wrapped in sad. "And I'd best be going." He gently drew me to him and I leaned on his chest. His heart beat so very hard. Another gentle movement and his warm mouth found mine for our very first kiss. He tasted of peppermint, which was not surprising. But there was something more than peppermint in that kiss.

Something like home.

He pulled back so that our lips were touching, but barely. His breath was warm and sweet. I closed my eyes, ready for another dreamy meeting of our mouths.

What was I thinking? The timing was all wrong for this. I pulled away, shaking my head to clear the fog.

"We'll still write?" I touched my fingers to my lips as if

to impress that sweet kiss upon them forever, as one might preserve a rose between the pages of a book, hoping against hope this first kiss wasn't to be our last.

He tugged at the bill of his cap. "You can write," he said. "But to tell you the truth, I'm not sure I'll be able to answer."

And with that, Charlie Hawley left. Taking a good chunk of my foolish heart right along with him.

❧ 4 ❧

A Chop Suey Day

June 24, 1919
Nearly to San Francisco

Dear Perilee,

*Today I have seen the ocean! Well, San Francisco
Bay, but I believe that counts. You cannot imagine it. I
thought it would be solid blue, like a flax field in bloom.
But it would take a whole slew of colors from a painter's
palette to capture it: purples and greens and grays and
blacks.*

Not only have I seen *the bay, I am* sailing *on it!
In a ferry that we boarded after the train stopped in
Oakland. The water rolls on as vast as Montana's sky
and yet we'll be across it in well under an hour. Imagine*

*that! Except for the cries of the gulls, it feels very much as
if I'm still on the train. Only I must say the ferry is a bit
more posh, with a separate tearoom for ladies. I shared
a pot of tea there with Maude—she's the ingénue of the
company.*

*Oh, I see the Ferry Building now! It's crowned with
an enormous clock tower standing like a lighthouse on
a lonely bluff. However, this tower guards the second-
busiest railroad station in the world. At least, that's what
the brochure here in the tearoom claims.*

*We are to disembark in a few minutes. I must close
for now.*

Exactly seventeen days had passed since I'd left Great Falls.
There'd been stops in Portland and Redding and some towns
whose names I'd already forgotten. Nothing in my journey
had prepared me for the big city of San Francisco.

Country mouse was the perfect description for me as I followed close on Maude's heels, terrified I would be separated
from the troupe and lost forever. I had never seen so many
people in one place before.

"Do close your mouth, Hattie," scolded Miss Clare. "It's
most unbecoming."

I closed my mouth but kept my eyes wide open. I didn't
want to miss a thing. Think of the pages I could fill in my
tablet! Oh, I couldn't wait to write about the swirls of people
and the sharp clean smell of seawater.

We exited the building onto a U-shaped plaza laid with
streetcar tracks. I glanced at Miss Clare to see if that was to

be our form of transport to the hotel, but she and Mr. Lancaster led us on to a stand of jitneys sufficient to carry a company of actors as well as their luggage and tools of the trade. As I was nudged forward to one of the vehicles, I spied a large white feather tipped in gray just in front of me. I quickly stooped to pick up this omen—appropriate for a young woman soaring into an unknown future—before being ushered into a car with Maude and a few others, including the new second boy, hired in Spokane to replace Cecil Hall. The second boy fell promptly asleep. Even though I was also done in from the long journey, I couldn't imagine closing my eyes and missing one speck of this amazing metropolis. Five Great Falls could fit within San Francisco's city limits, with space to spare. Each block we passed promised Grand Adventure. I had surely made the right decision in coming.

The streets were peppered with flower carts bursting with color. "It looks like one big bouquet!" I blurted out.

Maude smiled at my comment. "At Christmastime, it's awash in violets, ten cents a bunch. You'd love it then."

"I love it now!" Turning back to the window, I caught sight of both horse-drawn wagons and engine-powered vehicles maneuvering the streets in patterns of pure chaos. But I didn't witness one collision, or even a near miss. Clanging streetcar bells competed with newsboys shouting, "Dr. Dodge, *Titanic* survivor, in serious condition from suicide attempt. Read all about it!" Dapper policemen with white stripes running around their jacket cuffs and down their pant legs chanted, "Watch the trolleys, folks! Watch the traffic."

No matter which way I looked, there were people.

Businessmen in suits tipped their straw boaters to young women whose cloche hats covered stylish bobs. Mothers in wide-brimmed bonnets bustled hand in hand with boys in knickers and girls wearing such enormous satin bows atop their heads they looked like gift packages. And weaving in and out of all of the throngs were bareheaded laborers and deliverymen, some of them tiny Chinese with strange long pigtails bouncing on their backs. I imagined myself in one of Charlie's beloved airplanes, flying over this scene. From such heights, all these folks must look like popcorn kernels bouncing in a hot skillet.

Our first stop was the Fairmont Hotel, where Miss Clare and Mr. Lancaster would be residing for the run of the show. Perched atop Nob Hill, the Fairmont appeared to cover more ground than the entire town of Vida! This time I told *myself* to close my mouth, lest I look like a true hayseed. But it was hard not to gape a little at the sight of the formal garden and terrace at the rear. For a moment, I imagined myself at a palace in France or Italy. Then Miss Clare's decidedly American voice began to chatter in my ear.

"Are you listening, Hattie? I'm sending that trunk with you. It's got the costumes in need of repair."

I nodded attentively. Since our conversation in Mrs. Brown's kitchen, Miss Clare had not said another word about finding my replacement upon arrival in San Francisco. Not that I had found my calling, but I did not relish looking for another job right away. She rattled off a tediously long list of instructions—this gown needed the lace trim refreshed, that cape had a tear in the satin lining, Mr. Lancaster's tuxedo trousers were losing their hem.

"And my cranberry silk needs taking in again. Can you manage?" she asked.

"Yes, ma'am." The troupe had the night off, so I was confident I could get everything patched up and still find time to venture out to explore my new home.

After the stop at the Fairmont, our jitney rumbled along back to Stockton, heading toward the Hotel Cortez, where the rest of us were staying. Mrs. Brown would have been astonished to learn that one room cost the magnificent sum of $2.50 a week. Maude handed me my key and we stepped into the elevator. I couldn't help but smile at the memory of my first elevator ride, back at that hotel in Spokane. It had seemed impossible that a metal cage could travel up and down the way it did in the innards of a building. I was used to them by now, though my heart still skipped a bit every time an elevator began its upward lurch.

"I'm just one floor below you," Maude said, giving me her room number. "Knock if you need anything!"

When she stepped out at her floor, I felt a bit like a child who'd lost sight of her mother on a crowded street. Inhaling shakily, I called out "See you later" in the jauntiest manner I could muster.

After a short ride up, I was unlocking the door to my own room. It was as if I were unlocking a new life. I paused, savoring key in hand, before stepping through. My new lodgings were full of light and exotically decorated along a Spanish theme, and more than twice the size of my quarters at Mrs. Brown's. A gilt-framed print of none other than Cortez himself, rather than an assortment of Mrs. Brown's dour relatives, hung on the opposite wall. There were two chairs: a straight wooden one at the desk and a chubby upholstered one by the window, which would be the perfect reading spot. A twin bed and an armoire rounded out the furnishings. To think that the Fairmont would be even more luxurious than this! It was hard to feature.

I located the bathroom down the hall and freshened up. Since my possessions were few, I quickly had things stowed away and my room as homey as it could be. Uncle Chester's trunk, heavy with books, was to be delivered later from the station. I could already envision how I would arrange a row of select titles on the desk. For inspiration. And comfort. The gull feather I'd found outside the Ferry Building looked festive and hopeful in the desk's old inkwell; the letter from Ruby Danvers was propped up against it. I emptied my carry bag of tablets and pens with every intention of committing first impressions to paper but made the mistake of trying out the bed.

A knock roused me from my nap with a start. "Who's there?" I called, trying to shake the sleep from my voice. What time was it?

"It's Maude. Several of us are going for supper. Would you like to come along?"

I ran to the door and flung it open. "Can you give me a few minutes?"

"We'll wait for you in the lobby."

P,

    I will finish this letter with a description of my first San Francisco meal and new friend. Meal first: the lessers of the troupe (not my designation, but their own!) invited me on an excursion to Chinatown. If that were not adventure enough—Oh, the smells! The singsong language! The windows hung with plucked ducks and chickens!—we dined there, as well. I don't know the name of the restaurant—Maude called it a chow-chow—but we sat cheek by jowl with others likewise inspired to try foreign fare. I ordered something called chop suey, which reminded me of nights on the homestead when I threw together bits of this and that for a meal. It was tasty enough, but I can't see myself hurrying back soon. I did sample Maude's noodles doused with some kind of spicy gravy and that was good.

Maude Kirk has taken me under her wing. She is pert and lively and loves a good joke. It's very kind of her to befriend this little country mouse. Knowing there is someone to share a cup of coffee or commiserate with makes this big city seem cozier.

I will write again soon. You write, too!

Your Hattie

P.S. I've tucked in a picture post card of a Chinatown scene for the children.
P.P.S. If that was a mild tongue-lashing in your last letter, I tremble to think of a severe one. You and Charlie are in perfect agreement about my "foolhardy plan," as you so kindly put it.

39

SING FAT CO., INC.
THE FAMOUS ORIENTAL BAZAAR
S.W. CORNER CALIFORNIA ST. AND GRANT AVE.,
CHINATOWN
SAN FRANCISCO, CALIFORNIA
BRANCH: 548-550 SOUTH BROADWAY,
LOS ANGELES
美國全山正埠生菁公司

The evening's adventure with Maude emboldened me to explore my new home the next morning. It was part exploration and part reconnaissance. With the city guide I'd purchased at Owl Drug in hand, I started off after breakfast. The Orpheum Theater was on O'Farrell, between Stockton and Powell. I made my way there first to be certain I could find it. The theater was dark, of course; as I'd learned over the past weeks, the thespian world did not conceive of life before noon.

I'd determined a secondary target some four blocks past the theater. My personal Mecca was at the corner of Market and Kearny: a spot that was home to the three biggest newspapers in town. Half afraid I'd lose my nerve, I marched down the street as if I carried front-page news in my pocket. In no time, I passed the famous Lotta's Fountain and was rewarded with my first glimpse of Newspaper Row—the *Call,* the *Examiner,* and, right in front of me, loomed the Chronicle Building, a ten-story-high skyscraper. Its famous clock tower had been destroyed in the 1906 earthquake, but even without that dramatic finial, it was an impressive structure. I stood there a moment, taking it all in, allowing myself to fancify that someday I might walk into one of these buildings because I belonged there, that I'd have a desk and a typewriter and a pencil behind one ear, that I would hear the newsies touting my stories from the street corners. Read all about it!

One person after another stepped through the *Chronicle*'s great stone archway, topped with the newspaper's name spelled out in glass tubes that lit up at night. I played at guessing the occupation of each entrant pushing open the immense plate-glass doors. The skinny lad with the tweed cap might be an errand boy. The bareheaded man would be a reporter, in a rush to type up his scoop. And that portly fellow had to be an editor. You could just tell by the way he carried himself.

"After you, miss." A bow-tied gentleman was holding the door for me.

"Oh, I—" Why not go in? I'd come this far! "Thank you," I said. "Thank you very much."

No one questioned me as I stepped into the grand foyer.

In fact, there were such comings and goings, I doubt anyone even noticed me. Still, I felt somewhat like a child about to raid the cookie jar.

I found myself in front of the building directory. There it was: NEWSROOM. A little shiver went through me as I tried to imagine what such a place might be like. Would it be all clicking and clacking from busy typewriters? Reporters discussing the events of the world? Telephones ringing right and left? Whatever was up there, it was where I wanted to be. And all I had to do was get in that elevator, ride up a few floors and . . . and then what? Tell them about my pitiful little Honyocker's Homilies? At best, they'd laugh in my face. More likely, they'd pelt me with full ink bottles. I turned to leave.

A gaggle of girls not much older than me bubbled past. A redhead with the latest bob and a lopsided smile waved my way. "Are you here to apply for a telephone operator job, too?" she asked with a warm Southern drawl.

I looked over my shoulder to find the object of her inquiry. Without waiting for an answer, she snagged my arm. "Come on. We'll all head up together."

There was nothing to do but tag along, my worn brown oxfords thudding on the regal floors as their fashionable pointed heels smartly click-click-clicked.

"Golden Gate?" The Southern belle asked me as we settled in the elevator car.

"I'm sorry?"

"We're all grads of Miss Smith's Secretarial. Since I hadn't seen you around, I was guessing you'd gone to Golden Gate Business School."

I shook my head. "I'm not from here." My stomach sank, and it wasn't because of the elevator ride. These girls had training. Diplomas. And snazzy summer dresses, not an outmoded wool skirt topped with a once-white shirtwaist.

The elevator doors slid open. "Here we are," my new friend said. I let them all exit first, uncertain of what to do. I hadn't the smallest clue about managing a telephone switchboard, and I could only type with two fingers! I eased into the back corner of the car.

"You're not getting out, miss?" the operator asked.

Out of nervous habit, I touched Mother's watch pinned on my bodice. She'd had backbone, and Uncle Chester had believed I possessed some of that family starch. Well, I'd faced down stampeding horses on the prairie; I could surely face down fears about applying for a job. The elevator doors began to close.

"Wait!" I stepped forward. "I do want out."

The operator caught the doors before they shut and, luckily, before I lost my courage. "There you are, miss."

I thanked him and approached the receptionist's desk. The Miss Smith's girls were being shown into a big room, where they were given headsets with trumpet-shaped mouthpieces. The equipment looked like something out of a Jules Verne novel. I hung back until they were settled and the door between us swung closed.

"I'm here to apply for a job," I told the receptionist.

She looked at me over her glasses, eyebrows arched. With that look, my confidence nearly got on the train back to Great Falls. "You're late for the telephone test."

"Is there anything else?" I swallowed hard. "In the news-room, perhaps . . . ?" My voice trailed off.

"The newsroom!" The words were accompanied by a sharp bark of a laugh.

"I want to be a reporter."

"And I want to marry John D. Rockefeller." With a heavy exhale, she dismissed my aspirations. "Are you a high school graduate?"

I shook my head.

"Can you take shorthand? Type?" She clucked her tongue as I indicated no to both. "Well, what can you do?"

I can write, I wanted to say. But I didn't want to diminish my dream by speaking of it aloud to her. She might be all gussied up behind that desk, but I'd met her kind before—like the girls who'd mocked my hand-me-down dress at eighth-grade graduation or Traft Martin and his men, bully-ing the Germans back in Vida.

"I'm sorry." I turned to go.

"Sorry?" The woman looked puzzled.

"Yes. Sorry that your corset is too tight." It wasn't very nice of me, but there was no call for her to be so spiteful.

She leaned over her desk and stared right at me. And then she began to laugh. "You've got spunk," she said with a shake of her head. "I'll give you that." Chuckling, she rummaged around in one of the desk drawers. "Here." She pushed a form across to me.

I took it. "Cleaning staff?" Was this another of the good Lord's jokes? I thought I had left that behind.

"It's all there is right now. At least, for someone with your level of experience." The telephone on her desk trilled and she snatched up the receiver. "Take it or leave it," she mouthed to me before greeting the caller.

My hands shook as I filled out the form. She was still on the telephone when I handed it back to her, so she mouthed to me again. "We'll call you." I nodded and slunk away.

Outside, I claimed one of the benches by Lotta's Fountain, breathing as hard as if I'd been plowing a field. My first day in the big city had already taken more out of me than my first week on the homestead! Too done in to move, I sat watching all the people roiling thick and dark as a summer grasshopper hatch.

So many people. Was there room for one more? Was there room for me? I huddled on the bench, feeling small and foolish. Nearly as foolish as the day I'd gotten myself stuck to a frozen pump handle. Why on earth had I thought coming here was a good idea? I hadn't even liked that chop suey last night and it had set me back thirty-five cents. What if I never saw Perilee and Karl and the children again? Or Charlie? As I worked myself into a first-rate state of misery, a fluttering caught my attention. It was a snow-white feather, with soft frills of down rippling along the edges, spinning to a stop at the base of the fountain. Two feathers in two days. That verse from Matthew popped into my mind: "Are not two sparrows sold for one penny? Yet not one of them will fall to the ground outside your Father's care."

I got off the bench and picked it up. Somehow it had managed to avoid the armies of feet marching all around the fountain. It was still pristine white. That was a small miracle.

All right. I might be feeling a bit like Jonah, and this city might seem like that whale, ready to swallow me whole. But miracles were still possible. Tucking the feather into my pocketbook, I said a quiet prayer: "Dear Lord, with your help, Jonah made out okay, so I'm trusting I will, too. Amen."

Somewhere, a church bell chimed the hour. Time to make my way to the theater. I stuck my shoulders back. I hadn't been so naive as to think I'd break into the newspaper business my very first week. So why feel blue? I needed to give it time. Besides, there was another reason I'd been drawn here, and I must not forget that.

As soon as I could, I would make my way to Union Street and make the acquaintance of Ruby Danvers and, through her, come to know my uncle.

⟨ 5 ⟩

Ruby and Pearl

Not that I was a swimmer, but I'd heard that there was no sense in wading when planning a dip in the ocean. It was best to dive in and get the business of getting cold over with all at once. Today was my diving-in day. I was going to mail a post card to Charlie and then call on Ruby Danvers, and in that very order.

I gathered my things, reading over what I'd written one last time:

July 1, 1919

Charlie,

Here is where I first set foot in San Francisco. My room at the Hotel Cortez is "de luxe" and my new friend, Maude, has kindly pared this big city down to size for me.

Perilee wrote that you looked them up when you got to town. Knowing her, you left with a full stomach and something home-baked and tasty for later. I took your visit to the Muellers to be a hopeful sign that I might get a reply to this post card.

Hattie

THE FERRY BUILDING, SAN FRANCISCO, CALIFORNIA.

I sighed. There had been no answer to my two earlier cards. Perhaps the third time would be the charm. I could only hope.

The elevator door clanked open. When I stepped into the lobby, I bumped into Maude, off to have tea with her brother, Ned, before he went to work. She introduced us, saying, "Oh, I'm so glad you two have finally met. Ned's promised me he'll give you a tour of the *Chronicle*."

On the train to San Francisco, Maude had discovered me scribbling and badgered me until I showed her some of my writing. From that moment on, she had contrived to introduce me to her reporter brother.

"I couldn't impose," I told him.

"Not an imposition at all." He winked at me. "Even if it were, I'm used to being imposed upon. I am Maude's brother, after all." He ducked her swinging pocketbook with a chuckle.

"He's impossible," Maude said. "I wish we could stay and chat, but we're running late."

"*We're* late?" Ned raised his eyebrows. "I would like it duly noted that I have been pacing this lobby for a full twenty minutes."

"Oh, but I'm so worth waiting for, aren't I?" Maude took her brother's arm and they were off. I smiled after them. Their teasing brought to mind Charlie and me, at least the younger versions of Charlie and me.

"Good morning, Miss Hattie." Raymond greeted me from behind the front desk.

I returned the greeting, holding out the post card. "Would you please mail this?"

"Sure thing." He took it from me and then looked around for a moment.

"Outgoing mail slot. There." I pointed. I hadn't yet decided whether Raymond's confusion was due to age or to the bottle he sipped from with alarming regularity. "I'll be back later."

"Did you want to send a reply to that message?" he asked.

"Message?" I felt as confused as Raymond.

"The phone message?" At my blank look, he felt around in his pockets, then pulled out a slip of paper. "Guess I forgot to give it to you."

I took it from him. The *Chronicle* had finally called. Could I please drop by the newspaper at my earliest convenience? I certainly could! After my visit to Ruby Danvers. And—I avoided looking at myself in the lobby mirror—after some shopping. At the very least, I needed a new hat. Back in Vida, my shabby wardrobe was no different from anyone else's. Here, I stood out like a square of gingham in a fancy silk quilt.

Thanking Raymond, I took a deep breath and commenced my mission. The sidewalks seemed quite spirited, with American flags fluttering from storefronts in anticipation of the Fourth of July holiday. Several hotels were decked out with enormous red, white, and blue buntings. I would have enjoyed the sights even more had I not been carrying, in my moist hand, a slip of paper on which was written out Ruby Danvers' address. Maude had advised the most direct way to go, a kind gesture I did appreciate, but I now wished I had a more winding route to follow. Nervous at the thought of finally meeting Ruby Danvers, my stomach percolated like a pot of coffee.

Covington Apartment Hotel, where she lived, was less than a mile from the Cortez, but I splurged on the nickel fare to ride the cable car up to Union from Mason. No sense undoing my freshened-up hair and clean shirtwaist with a sweaty walk up a hill. First impressions iron permanent creases, Aunt Ivy had often warned me. If I must bring sad news, it wouldn't do except to look my best. Though my best was hardly beguiling; no one my age wore such long skirts.

"Union!" the grip called out, and I quickly shook off my fashion daydreams and stepped down from the cable car. In for a penny, in for a pound; I would not turn back now.

Not ten steps from the cable car tracks, I found another gull's feather, pure white along the shaft but deepening to the gray of Rooster Jim's horses along the vane. I glanced up. It was almost as if someone—Uncle Chester?—was up there, scattering feathers before me like bread crumbs. With a lighter heart, I tucked the treasure into my pocketbook.

The two- and three-story flats lining either side of Union Street looked like grand ships, with bay-window prows sailing out over the sidewalks. In several of the windows, contented felines curled up on becushioned seats. I moved at a snail's pace as much to take in the new sights as to try to calm my nerves, but each step set my heart to skittering faster and faster. Too soon I was crossing Jones. There it was: 1074 Union. The address from which the letter in my pocketbook had been sent.

The solid brick building and heavy entry doors furnished a dramatic contrast to my image of Ruby Danvers' daintiness. Inside, the foyer was garlanded with faded crepe-paper streamers and the aroma of many years of onions cooking. My shoes tap-tapped across the worn tiled floor to the directory. R. DANVERS was the name next to apartment 302. Third floor.

Too jangled to latch myself into a metal cage for an elevator ride, I opted for the stairs. With each tread, I rehearsed my introduction: *Mrs. Danvers? I am Hattie Brooks, and I bear sad news about my uncle. Mrs. Danvers? I am Hattie Brooks, and I bear—* Wait. Perhaps instead, I should say *my* late *uncle.* That way she'd know right off that Uncle Chester was gone.

No. Too harsh. I would stick with my original script. Like the actors in the Varietals, I practiced my lines as I climbed up and up on increasingly rubbery legs.

I found myself in front of apartment 302. I knocked. And waited. Knocked again. Waited again.

"She's at work," a female voice behind me announced.

I turned to see a tiny old woman, no taller than a fence rail. Her white braid wound around her head in a flyaway tangle.

"I should have called ahead." Just because I had the day off was a foolish reason to assume Ruby Danvers would be at home. "Is there somewhere I could leave a message?"

The old lady squinted at me. "When's your birthday?"

What a question! But I wasn't about to be rude to this granny. "October twenty-eighth."

She sucked in her ill-fitting teeth. "Who keeps an arrow in his bow and if you prod him lets it go? A fervent friend and subtle foe. It is the Scorpio."

"Yes. Well. I best be going."

"You. You're a Scorpio. Many great writers are."

Now she had my interest. "Like who?" I didn't know much about astrology except that Aunt Ivy called it unchristian.

"Voltaire. Robert Louis Stevenson. Stephen Crane." She chuckled. "And Marie Antoinette."

My hand went to my throat. "Well, three out of four isn't bad."

Her head tipped back and a lion's roar of a laugh escaped. "You've got wit, that you have." She motioned me close. "Scorpios are trustworthy. Not like some as have rapped on that very door." She jigged her white head toward apartment 302. "So I can tell you. She's got herself a fancy job for that Mr. Stuart Wilkes. Personal assistant, mind you." Her eyebrows waggled. "La-di-dah."

Was my astrologer friend in her right mind? The odds seemed against it, but what did I have to lose? "Where is Mr. Wilkes' office?"

"Pacific Building. Downtown."

It wasn't far from the Orpheum. I recalled passing it. "Thank you. I'll try her there."

"You can try her, but not as much as she will try you." The old lady held her hand up, as a pastor might when giving a blessing. "But you're a scorpion. You'll manage just fine."

I smiled uneasily and backed away, giving my new friend an uncertain wave from the elevator car. As the door slid between us, she turned and I could hear her mutter, "Figaro, you darned cat. Where have you got off to this time?"

Out on the street, I consulted my Owl Drug map to make certain I was headed in the right direction. I opted to save the nickel carfare this time; I would rather apply it to the purchase of a cool soda at the end of my wanderings. As I walked, I puzzled over that peculiar little old lady. I'd certainly never met anyone like her before! And that is precisely why you came to San Francisco, I reminded myself. To do the unusual. And meet the unusual.

After a brisk walk, I found myself at the Pacific Building and stepped inside to study the directory. Accountants. Brokers. Detective agencies! Not one but two were listed: WEST COAST DETECTIVE AGENCY, THOMAS L. GRAY, GENERAL MANAGER, CHARGES REASONABLE, and GIGNAC SECRET SERVICE BUREAU, LUCIEN K. GIGNAC, PRESIDENT, DETECTIVE BUSINESS TRANSACTED THROUGHOUT THE WORLD. Imagine two detective agencies in the same place. Back in Arlington, there wasn't even one. Truth to tell, such services weren't needed, not with Aunt Ivy and the Ladies' Guild keeping watchful eyes and sharp ears trained on the rest of the community.

I kept scanning the list. Could my old-lady friend have sent me on a fool's errand? Insurance. Underwriters. There! WILKES, STUART, ESQ. 7TH FLOOR. Now I hesitated. Perhaps I should simply send a note. What if Ruby was in the middle of something? The news I had was hardly fit to share in a public place like an office. I reached into my pocketbook, feeling around for the letter, my fingers brushing the feather I'd found on my way to Ruby Danvers' apartment. Okay, Uncle Chester. I'll do it.

"Seventh floor," I said to the elevator operator, squeezing into the nearly full car.

Three quick stops and we were there. I stepped out, glancing first right and then left.

"What office are you looking for?" the elevator operator asked. When I told him, he said, "Around the corner. End of the hall. You can't miss it."

And I couldn't. The office door was the fanciest portal I'd ever seen in my life. All oiled rosewood, carved with curlicues and oak leaves. It would take a giant's knock on that door to be heard inside. I took a deep breath and turned the gleaming brass knob.

The interior was as elaborate as the door, decorated with dark ornate woods and glass-fronted bookcases and statues and framed citations and diplomas. A blond woman wearing pince-nez spectacles glanced up from her work.

"Are you Ruby Danvers?" I asked.

She pointed to a nameplate on her desk that said MRS. HOLM. "Mrs. Danvers is on her way to lunch. Do you have an appointment?"

I shook my head and patted my pocketbook. "I have something to return to her."

At that, Mrs. Holm picked up some sort of handset, and the next thing I knew, I was being escorted into an office as light and feminine as the outer sanctum was ponderous and masculine. Her back was to me, and she was slipping into hat and wrap, obviously preparing to leave, but she was just as I had imagined: delicate and small, a dainty magnolia flower to my coarse gumbo lily. The only thing I hadn't imagined was the red hair.

"Mrs. Danvers? A young lady to see you." Mrs. Holm announced me, then disappeared.

Ruby Danvers turned to face me, a quizzical expression on her face. "I'm sorry. Have we met?"

I stepped into the room. "No. Not exactly. I have something that belongs to you." I rummaged in my bag, retrieving letter and token.

She reached behind her for a chair and sat. Hard. "Close the door," she said.

I did so, taking a deep breath before reciting the lines I'd rehearsed. "I am Hattie Brooks, niece to Chester Wright." I cleared my throat. "The late Chester Wright."

She motioned me near, holding out her hand. I laid my deliveries across her gloved palm.

She shook the token out of the letter and into that same palm. She lifted it to her cheek, looking even more fragile.

"When I didn't hear from Chester right away, I knew it was bad news. One way or another." She closed her eyes for a moment, then gazed at me again. "It was very kind of you to come. It could not have been an easy thing to do."

"I am so sorry for your loss." I recited words I'd heard Aunt Ivy and her friends say at times like this, twisting my pocketbook strap in my hands.

"I lost Chester a long time ago." She uncurled her fingers and studied the token. "Silly of me to have kept this. And even sillier to have sent it."

There didn't seem to be anything for me to say to that. I stepped back toward the door. "I can see you're on your way out."

"That can wait." She pointed to a chair arranged in cozy proximity to hers. "Please sit down."

We settled ourselves. "Would you mind . . ." She paused. "Would it be difficult for you to tell me about this place in Montana that stole my Chester's heart?"

I explained about his bequeathing me the homestead claim in the will. About my leaving Iowa to try to finish proving up on it. "I certainly bit off more than I could chew, but the thought of a home of my own—" I hugged myself. "Well, to an orphan, that's pretty close to having a real family."

"And you didn't stay?" she asked.

"Couldn't." I told her the whole story, starting at the beginning, with the letter from Uncle Chester.

She was a good listener, asking a gentle question here and there, encouraging me to keep talking.

"You didn't!" she said, when I told her about getting frozen to the pump handle.

"I did. Thank goodness Chase came along to rescue me." That led me to tell her all about Perilee and Karl and the children, and my other prairie friends. I told her about digging fence posts and the barn fire. And, perhaps because we shared a bond of sorrow, I even told her about the Spanish influenza and losing our little Mattie Magpie. "I nursed her day and night," I said, my voice straining around the pain. "Perilee's other girls got better. But I couldn't save Mattie." This was the first time I'd uttered these words aloud.

She slipped over and knelt beside me, taking my hands in hers. "You mustn't blame yourself, dear Hattie. It is so very clear how much you love those children."

I soaked up her kind sympathy. How odd that I'd just met her and yet it felt as if our hearts had always known one another.

She dabbed at her eyes and blew her nose with a lacy handkerchief. "A good cry always leaves me famished, isn't that silly?"

I shrugged, trying to blow my nose as delicately as she had.

"Have you lunched yet?" she asked.

"No—"

"Oh, I imagine a young woman like you has plans." She stood up, smoothing her skirts.

"Well, I did have plans to do some shopping." I glanced down at my clothes. "What wears in Vida doesn't wear in San Francisco."

She clapped her hands together. "Shopping! Just the thing to boost the spirits." She took her bag down from a hook behind her desk and slipped it on her arm. Then she slipped her arm around mine. "I feel we are going to be best friends, Hattie." She paused again, looking sad. "Having you near would make up for being so far from Pearl."

At my questioning face, she continued. "My daughter." She touched her neck, then laughed softly. "I'd forgotten— the clasp on the locket is being repaired. I usually wear her here, close to my heart." She turned her gaze away from me, to the window. "She's living with Mother right now. I need to work, and jobs are hard to come by in Santa Clara. A few weeks ago, a friend suggested this job with Mr. Wilkes and I couldn't say no."

I knew all too well about taking jobs out of necessity. "Oh, I hope I get to meet her."

Ruby laughed. "Of course, every mother thinks her child is perfect. But Pearl is the sweetest thing. Only ten, but so grown-up and serious." She shook her head. "When you come to tea, I'll bring out the photo albums."

When I come to tea! Finding Ruby Danvers was like chancing upon another Perilee. What luck for an orphan to find a home in two such big and kind hearts. Ruby nudged me toward the door. "I hear the Emporium calling us! Lunch first, then some serious shopping."

Not only would Ruby not let me pay for my lunch, she insisted on treating me to my first big city ensemble. She picked out a summer dress of orange and cream, with a cascade of kick pleats that started above the knee, topped by a smart jacket in a warm yellow flower print, with ruffles at the elbows. I didn't even recognize myself in the mirror when I tried it on.

Ruby gave me a smile of approval. "That's the kind of dress a girl wears when she's going places," she said.

I smiled at that. Even if one of the places she was going was to a job as a cleaning woman! Oh, well.

We tussled over the purchase of a hat. She wanted to buy me a saucy orange number with a bill that swooped to small wings behind my ears. It was dreamy, but well out of my budget. "No, I can't let you pay for this, too." I settled on a simple butterscotch cloche for the sensible price of $2.25. I also bought myself a well-priced worsted navy walking dress, with buttons the size of dinner plates.

When it came time to pay for our purchases, I brought out my wrinkled and hard-earned bills.

"Oh, dear, that is so old-fashioned. You really need to open a checking account. Next time we're out, I'll help you." Ruby turned to the clerk. "I didn't plan on shopping today and my checkbook's at home."

"That's no problem, ma'am. If you'll tell me which bank holds your account, I can provide you with a counter check." Ruby named the bank and the clerk brought out the proper check blank. I watched carefully as she filled in her account number and then signed her name with a flourish. Even her signature was stylish.

"It's been lovely, darling, but I best get back or Mr. Wilkes will wonder what he's paying me for!" She kissed my cheek as we parted. "You look fabulous." She'd talked me into wearing my new outfit out of the store. Though shorter hemlines were all the rage, it was hard to get used to seeing so much of my legs. Thank goodness Aunt Ivy was a thousand miles away! I could only imagine the lecture she'd give me. My new outfit made me feel modern. Ready for anything! I looked at my shabby oxfords. I was especially ready for footwear that matched the new me.

Ruby caught me staring at my feet. "Head over to Praeger's. You'll find good prices on the latest shoes."

After the stop at Praeger's, my pocketbook was another four dollars lighter, but my step was lighter, too, in my new brown tango shoes with the smart buckle across the front of my ankle. In fact, I felt smart head to toe, smart enough to stroll right over to the *Chronicle* to take that darned cleaning job. Lots of people had started at the bottom. Like Horatio Alger's Ragged Dick. And Henry Ford. And even—dare I think it?—Nellie Bly.

Armored in my new wardrobe, I marched straight from Praeger's to the *Chronicle,* the shopping bags with my old clothes banging against my legs. If nothing else, Miss Tight

Corset would appreciate my newly adopted San Francisco style. I pushed through the great glass doors and fairly pranced across the grand foyer to the elevator bank. Today, cleaning woman; tomorrow, ace reporter!

The doors opened and I stood aside to let the passengers exit.

"Miss Brooks?" A male voice stopped me. "I didn't expect to see you so soon."

It was Maude's brother, Ned.

{❧ 6 ❧}

Headlines and Hard Truths

Whatever you are, be a good one.

—Abraham Lincoln

Ned crossed the lobby to meet me. "Are you here for that tour already? I wasn't expecting you, but I'm waiting on a source to get back to me, so your timing's impeccable."

Of all the luck. Why did I have to run into *him*? He was a reporter. Of course a reporter would ask questions. "Yes. No. I mean, I wouldn't impose on such short notice."

Panic must have been apparent on my face. He stepped closer and took my parcels. "It's really no bother. Come along."

I tried one more time. "Honestly, I just stopped by to—" To what? My brain was not giving my mouth any assistance.

"And I'm delighted you did. Off we go now."

I said a quick prayer that our wanderings would not take me anywhere near Miss Tight Corset. I responded to Ned's warm smile with a tepid one of my own. Only I could get myself into such a pickle!

"Your secret is out," he said.

"Secret?" Could this get any worse?

He nodded. "Maude told me that you're published yourself. Honyocker's Homilies. Sounds like something I'd enjoy reading."

I stopped. "Promise you won't tell anyone. About my homilies." There'd probably be bruises later where I clenched his arm. "Promise."

"Not only are you a writer, you're modest, to boot." He drew an X across his chest. "Promise. Now come on." We stepped into the grating elevator. Up we went until the operator announced, "Newsroom." Ned towed me out. We weaved our way through half a dozen young men milling about in the hallway. "They're waiting for that big break," Ned said.

"You mean they don't work here?" I asked.

"No, but they want to." He glanced over his shoulder. "It happened to me, it could happen to them," he added.

"What happened to you?"

"This." He slipped a press card from his breast pocket. "I was part of that crowd, too, but I hung around and hung around until one day all the reporters were out on assignment and Monson—he's the managing editor—hollered for a stringer. I got to Monson first, snagged the story, and"—he grinned—"the job of my dreams."

"That gives me the chills." It also gave me hope about landing the job of *my* dreams.

We stepped around a corner into a well-lit space abuzz with activity and energy. "Welcome to the madhouse!" Ned motioned me forward. A parquet floor checkerboarded beneath our feet to a row of glassed-in offices, transom windows ajar above the closed doors. A double row of desks marched up the center of the room. Each desk's occupant clicked and clacked away at the typewriter in front of them, occasionally ripping a page out of the machine and calling, "Boy!" That command summoned an office boy who took the sheet and ran it, Ned explained, "Off to the copy readers."

I could hear Miss Clare's voice in my head saying, "Close your mouth, Hattie." But there was so much to take in! The staccato rhythm of the typewriter keys pounded into my very being. No salty sea air in here: I inhaled a mist of eraser dust, cigarette smoke, and excitement. I glanced down the rows of desks across a sea of suit coats dotted with the occasional shirtsleeve and started when I saw a hat that Maude would've envied. And that fabulous hat sat atop a head of hair the color of Praeger's best black patent leather shoes. A woman! In the newsroom.

"Who's that?" I whispered to Ned.

"Miss Marjorie D'Lacorte." He grimaced. "Otherwise known as the Tiger Woman."

At that moment, an office boy sidled up to Miss D'Lacorte's desk, stopping an arm's length away. "Excuse me, ma'am—"

The Tiger Woman extended one red-polished claw into the air, signaling quiet. She kept typing, one-handed.

"Mr. Monson wonders—" the hapless boy started again.

"Monson wonders!" the Tiger Woman roared. "That'll be the day. Now scram and let me finish this. I've got a smashing lead, and I don't want to lose it." The boy scrammed and Miss D'Lacorte tapped on the typewriter keys with military rhythm.

"I'll introduce you two another time," Ned said.

My innards sloshed like soup at the thought of being introduced to her. Ever. I wasn't sure my head would survive the meeting.

Ned led the way back to the elevator, and we jostled and banged our way to the next stop. Over the commotion, he told me more about Miss D'Lacorte. "Marjorie is the *Chronicle*'s version of Nellie Bly. With a little Captain Bligh thrown in for good measure," he added, referring to the cruel commander of the HMS *Bounty*. "She's a good writer, but a hard egg."

I wondered if a woman in a man's world could be anything but a hard egg. That thought gave me pause, as I certainly wasn't the Tiger Woman type. Maybe the roar came with experience.

The noisy elevator had been relative peace and quiet compared to our destination. "Watch out for boys with turtles," Ned shouted as we stepped into an enormous room jampacked with thundering machines.

"What?" I was certain I'd misheard him. Then a young man dashed by, pushing a wheeled rectangular cart. We barely missed colliding. "Turtles!" I exclaimed.

"And nothing slow about them." Ned motioned me over

to a stationary turtle. "This is the chase," he said, indicating a heavy metal frame atop the turtle-cart. "The compositors take slugs of type from the linotypes over there—" He pointed to two rows of massive machines, groaning and roaring in operation.

They could have been dragons, crouched on sturdy haunches, the sunlight barely piercing their smoky exhalations, ready at any moment to spread colossal scaly wings for flight. The only things to remind me that these were not dragons, though no less fantastical, were the operators' brass spittoons gleaming brightly on the floor next to each machine.

"And then they lock them into the chase, here, before rolling the turtles to the press room," Ned finished his explanation.

I couldn't help covering my ears as we walked the entire length of the floor. We exited through a steel door, and the immediate quiet in the stairwell was pure joy to my throbbing head. "How do the men stand the din, day after day?" I asked.

"Well, it's part of the job. So is shaking out bits of linotype lead from their clothes each night. But I don't imagine one fellow in there would trade his job for anything. The pen is mightier than the sword and all that." Ned once again offered his arm for our journey to yet another floor, where a huge wave of inky perfume rolled over and around us. Again, it was noise on top of noise as presses clattered and ground, paper rolling off great reels like black-and-white yard goods. I smiled to think of making a quilt out of all this newsprint.

We moved from the noisiest rooms to the quietest. Not that the editorial floor was all that quiet. People were calling out to one another, and in the pauses between voices and ringing telephones, a squadron of blue pencils scritch-scratched over reporters' copy.

"Now you've seen it all," Ned said. "Almost." He gestured down with his thumb. "There's still the morgue."

A chill shot through me as we retraced our footsteps even though I knew a newspaper morgue housed not bodies but back issues. "Do you have to work here to use the morgue?"

Ned rubbed his dapper moustache. "Why? Is there someone whose checkered past you wish to uncover?" He guided me to the right. "We're going to turn at the end of the hall there."

I forced myself to keep my tone as light as his. "A lady never snoops." But I had been thinking about pasts—specifically, Uncle Chester's.

He laughed aloud. "I'm sure you're right about that. Ladies don't." He pulled open the next door for me. "But reporters—both male and female—surely do. It's part of the job."

"Well, Miss Brooks."

I turned at the vaguely familiar voice. "Oh. Good afternoon, ma'am," I said to Miss Tight Corset.

Ned wore a quizzical expression on his face. "You two know each other?"

"Hardly." Miss Tight Corset pursed her lips. "But I may have the pleasure"—she said this as if she meant the complete opposite—"should Miss Brooks accept our offer of employment."

"You're coming to work here?" Ned straightened his tie. "That's the bee's knees. Which department?"

I made my eyes look as pitiful as possible, sending Miss Tight Corset a silent message not to tell.

With a brisk nod, she took my arm. "No chitchatting. There are papers to be filled out. You can socialize on your own time." With that, I took my parcels back from Ned and she escorted me away. I could have hugged her! I gave Ned a quick glance and a wave over my shoulder.

You would have thought I was applying for a job as publisher of the newspaper, there were that many forms to fill out. Miss Tight Corset turned off her desk lamp and was gathering her things up to go home for the night by the time I finished.

She gave them a quick once-over. "This all looks fine. Can you start tomorrow night?"

The job was the graveyard shift, ten p.m. to six a.m. Worse than farmer's hours. But much better than farmer's pay! Better than a wardrobe mistress's wage, too. "I need to give my current employer a day or so notice."

With a sigh she flipped through the day calendar on her desk. "Hmm. Thursday's the third, and it seems pointless to start the day before a holiday. I guess you'll have to start Monday. I'll tell the night watchman to expect you. Come to the front door. There'll be a work smock for you in the custodial room."

I gathered my parcels and smoothed the skirt of my new dress. "Thank you. For everything."

"Believe it or not, I was young once, too." She settled her hat on her head. "Good luck with your young man."

She was out the door before I could correct her mistake about Ned. No matter. I took a deep breath. I had a job at a newspaper! I did a little twirl, right there in the employment office. It wasn't the job of my dreams—far from it—but it was a job for a newspaper. I only hoped it wouldn't be too long from heavy lifting to headlines! I hummed while waiting for the elevator to arrive. Though I wasn't crazy about the thought of walking to work at night, the late shift would mean it would be easier to avoid Ned. With luck, he'd never know his sister's friend was dusting the desk he sat at each day.

The elevator dinged and I readied myself to step inside. And found myself face to face with Ned. Again!

"Fancy meeting you here." He winked. "Everything all set with the new job?"

"Yes. Quite set."

"Want me to show you where the steno pool is?" He stepped aside to make room for me in the crowded car.

"Oh, no thanks." This wasn't exactly a fib. I didn't *say* I worked in the steno pool; he assumed that.

"I have a fine idea to go with that fine new dress."

My cheeks burned hot with the attention.

"We're practically coworkers. I'd say that calls for a celebration. Do you have plans for dinner?"

I shifted my feet. My new shoes pinched a bit. "It's only a starter job."

"Well, you have to eat, don't you? Have you been to the New Delmonico?"

"No, but I couldn't—"

He shook his finger at me. "What you really mean to say is 'Yes, I'd love to, Ned.'" Then he cocked his head and batted his lashes, doing his best imitation of a pup with big brown eyes. I couldn't help it. I started laughing.

"I'm taking that as a yes."

Why not? A pleasant dinner with a new friend beat out a grilled cheese sandwich from the corner diner any day. "It's a yes."

Once again, he took my bags from me, and we stepped outside, brushed by a warm summer breeze. Somewhere in the distance, a tuba oompahed, and strains of a John Philip Sousa march filled the air.

Ned and I chattered the entire way to the restaurant. He was full of stories. Summer holidays with Maude. Pranks he'd pulled in college. Stateside war duty stuck typing reports. "The only good thing about that desk job was that my boss was an old newspaper man. Drilled the 'who, what, where, when, why, and how' into me, that's for sure. Ah, here we are."

New Delmonico's was the swankiest restaurant I'd ever been in. It would take more than a chic dress and new hat to make me look like I belonged. Ned took it all in stride, greeting the maître d' by name and shaking his hand.

After we were seated, I did my best to nudge my shopping bags under the table while Ned ordered each of us an iceberg lettuce salad with shrimp and Russian dressing to start. He went for the roast beef main course; I chose the chicken. A waiter swooped by, balancing a tray laden with glistening wedges of chocolate cream pie. I made a note to leave room for dessert.

"So. When do I get to read some of your writing?" Ned asked.

I concentrated on sweetening my iced tea. "Oh, it's not very good."

"Quantity grows quality," he pronounced. "And Maude says you're always scribbling away in every spare moment at the theater. That's the first sign that you have the disease."

"Disease?" I didn't realize Maude had seen me writing backstage. I thought I'd been so discreet.

He nodded solemnly. "Yes. It strikes the least suspecting. It begins with rewriting letters to friends before mailing them off."

How did he know I did that?

"And then it moves on to challenging oneself to find twelve ways to describe a"—he glanced around the café— "a tomato aspic." He sighed heavily and dramatically. "And finally, the patient succumbs."

Ned had a knack for tickling my funny bone. I laughed. "To what, pray tell?"

"To a life of writing."

"I wish." I picked up my fork and set it back down. "Tell me about your job. What's it like to be a real reporter?"

His eyes lit up. "No two days are ever the same! And you never know when something's going to blow. You have to think on your feet. And you have to trust that, no matter how dry your brain is, once you press your fingers to those typewriter keys, some kind of story is going to emerge." He tapped the white tablecloth with his fingertips as if typing. "Besides, even if it's darned good, the copy readers will rip it to pieces." He rolled his eyes.

The waiter arrived with our salads and we dealt with napkins and salt and pepper and tasting and such for several minutes. I savored the cool flavors in my mouth—lettuce, shrimp, and tangy dressing—as I savored the thought of being a reporter, like Ned. The thought was equally as delicious as the salad.

"So is Miss D'Lacorte the only woman reporter at the paper?"

He dabbed at his mouth with his napkin. "General reporter, yes. There are two gals on the fashion and society desk." He crooked his pinky. "Silk dresses, silver spoons, and all that."

We munched in silence for a few moments.

"Well, does she have to be the only woman reporter?" I reached for my glass of water. "Is there room for another?"

"Like a certain Miss Brooks?" he asked.

I felt my cheeks go hot again. But I stood my ground. "Why not?"

"Indeed." He leaned his elbows on the table, resting his chin on his hands, and looked straight at me. "Why not?"

"So what would it take, do you think?"

His expression grew thoughtful. I was grateful to him for taking me seriously. "You'd need a story. It doesn't have to be page one–worthy, but it must be the kind of story that makes you stand out. Something only you could write."

I traced the fork tines through the dribs of salad dressing on my plate. "I don't suppose anyone here wants to read about my homestead exploits."

"Not that they wouldn't want to, of course," he said gallantly. "But it's been done. You need something new. Something different. Something with a San Francisco connection. A hook to *this* city."

An idea began bubbling like soup stock on low heat. "It could be about anything?" I asked. Or anybody, I added to myself.

"Sure." He waved the waiter over to clear away our salad plates. "Whatever it is, you can count me in to help."

The conversation shifted as we enjoyed our main courses. Even though I'd tried, I had left no room for dessert. Ned had a cup of coffee, and then he paid the bill.

"Thank you," I said, hesitating to even give voice to the request on the tip of my tongue. Was it proper? Was it right? Would it even be news? Well, a fish certainly doesn't jump in the skillet by itself, does it? As Ned said, I needed a hook. And it could be that I had one. I'd never know if I didn't do some digging. "You've been so nice, I hate to impose further—"

"Impose away, fair lady!" He bowed his head at me across the table.

"Could you get me permission to use the morgue?" I ducked my eyes down. "And would you?"

"Could and would," he said, pulling my chair out. "You let me know when." He took my hand in his warm firm grasp and shook it. "I look forward to it. And I look forward to seeing you around the Chronicle Building!"

I forced a smile, imagining him catching me with a bucket of suds and a mop. Not if I can help it, I thought. Not if I can help it.

7

Piecing Together a New Life

When life throws you scraps, make a quilt.

—Anonymous

A new act had joined the Varietals: Harry Horowitz and his Happy Hounds. The resultant increase in wear and tear on costumes (the Hounds were not Happy unless chewing holes in performers' trousers, skirts, and an alarming assortment of other stage garb) required that my last day as wardrobe mistress be postponed until Sunday—the day before I started at the *Chronicle.*

The deluge of doggy-related disasters had kept me from accepting either of the invitations I'd received for Fourth of July activities. Ned and Maude had invited me to a party at a friend's home, and Ruby planned a picnic at the Presidio.

I celebrated our nation's independence by patching a hole in the seat of Mr. Lancaster's best tuxedo pants. By Sunday afternoon, I might have still been mending costumes had Mr. Lancaster not issued an ultimatum that if he found one more tooth mark on any costume, prop, or personal effect, he would sell the Hounds to the nearest Chinese restaurant— "toot sweet." Harry promptly produced muzzles for his pooches, and I was given leave to, well, leave.

Miss Vera Clare had fussed a bit about my resignation. "Your timing is most inconvenient," she said, apparently having forgotten her plan to hire a new wardrobe mistress upon our arrival here. But she did present me with a going-away gift.

"It's lovely!" The package contained an elegant journal, the kind I drooled over but could never afford. "Thank you so much."

She fussed with her hair. "Make sure you spell my name correctly when you write about me," she said. But a wink accompanied her words.

There were hugs and good wishes all around from the actors as they straggled in for the matinee. I took a hug from Maude, too, even though we'd still see each other at the hotel. After shopping around, I realized that what had seemed extravagant to my newly-arrived-from-Great-Falls-self was a more than reasonable rate for San Francisco, so I was keeping my lodgings at the Cortez.

I hurried from the theater to Ruby's apartment. She'd invited me for Sunday supper, since our picnic plans had fallen through. I'd dressed up for the occasion in my new navy walking dress, set off nicely by my new butterscotch cloche. When I arrived and stepped into the building's lobby, I noticed a funny little egg-shaped man wearing a straw hat and an impossibly pastel summer-weight suit. My astrologer friend had him cornered, wagging her head and muttering, "The goat does scheme for fortune and fame; beware, beware his game."

The man nodded. "But of course. Of course." He wiped his brow with a handkerchief, catching sight of me at that moment.

"Oh, *pardonnez-moi, mademoiselle.*"

But the elevator door opened and I popped in. "Sorry!" I made a sympathetic face as the gate clanged shut. After a morning of wrangling with Harry's Hounds, I had no strength for rescuing complete strangers from dotty old ladies.

"Oh, I'm so glad you're here." Ruby swooped me into a lily of the valley–scented hug. "I have a wonderful surprise."

I hung up my hat and pocketbook and followed her into the apartment. A small mountain of brown-paper parcels teetered precariously on the heavy settee. A georgette party dress in a warm apricot, with price tag still attached, was draped over a leather club chair.

"You've been on a shopping spree." Three Emporium hatboxes leaned against a mahogany desk. The stodgy furniture seemed at odds with Ruby's personal style. I would have thought her to possess delicate pieces, say a wicker settee or rosewood chairs with intricate carvings and cabriole legs. I lightly brushed my fingers against one of the dress's apricot ruffles. "This is so pretty," I said, though it seemed fancy for office wear, even Mr. Wilkes' office.

She laughed. "That's what happens when I get my paycheck and good news at the same time." She moved aside the packages on the settee. "Sit down. I'm so excited, I don't know what to do first." She looked like a child catching sight of a well-stuffed Christmas stocking.

I sat, smiling back at her even though I didn't know what I was smiling about. Her joy was simply contagious.

She started to sit, too, then stopped. "Oh, I bought the most delicious cookies. I'll be right back."

While she was in the kitchen, I took stock of the room. No fewer than three cut-glass vases brimmed with flowers. Though the furniture in the room seemed out of scale for its occupant, at least Ruby hadn't tried to feminize it with tatted doilies. That was all the rage among Aunt Ivy's friends, giving the impression that a lace blizzard had blown through. This room was bare of such fussiness. It was bare of books, too, which surprised me. With Uncle Chester being such a reader, I would've thought she might own at least one small bookcase, stocked perhaps with *Sister Carrie,* or *To Have and to Hold,* or even one of Frank L. Baum's fantastic Wizard of Oz tales. The only book I saw was a heavy Bible, open on a tiger-oak table opposite me.

"Here we are." Ruby carried in a tray with two tall glasses and a plate of those wonderful macaroons I'd already discovered at Schubert's Bakery on Fillmore. She placed the tray on a butler table, then settled in a chair opposite me.

I took a cookie and sat back. "You'd best tell me your news or we'll both explode."

Ruby clasped her hands. "I don't know where to begin."

Suddenly, she was pulling a handkerchief from her sleeve and dabbing her eyes.

"Are you all right?" I leaned toward her.

"Yes." She held up her hand. "I'm so happy. So wonderfully happy." She sniffled and then went on. "You can't imagine how hard it has been since Mr. Danvers died. My dear mother lived with us and it fell to me to keep us all going, and then, with Pearl taking ill—" She stopped and looked at me. "Oh, that was thoughtless of me. If anyone could imagine hard times, it would be you."

"Don't. I know what you mean." I indicated for her to continue.

She put away her handkerchief. "That's why it is so special to be able to share this news with you. Pearl is coming home!"

"Oh, that's wonderful!" This dear woman certainly deserved such news. "When? For how long?"

"In August." She put her hand to her heart. "Things are finally going well for me. So perhaps she'll stay for good."

I flew to her. "Oh, that must be an answer to prayer." We hugged and she kissed me on the cheek. When we pulled away, I was carrying her lily of the valley scent.

She picked up one of the paper parcels. "I was hoping you would help me make a quilt for Pearl. To help this"— she swept her gaze around the apartment—"feel more like home."

I put my hands on my hips. "I'll have you know I am the queen bee of quilters!" That might have been a bit of an exaggeration, but thanks to Perilee's instruction, I could piece and stitch with the best of them. Hot tears pricked my eyes, however, to think of the last quilt I'd made: Mattie's Magic. I quickly shook away those tears and held out my hand for the parcel in Ruby's. "Let's see what we've got to work with."

While we went through the packages, Ruby fretted about my new job at the *Chronicle*.

"I know you'll be running the newsroom in no time," she said. Her expression was so confident and sincere, I almost believed her. "But I hate thinking of you going to work at that time of night." She reached for her pocketbook and brought out a five-dollar bill. "Use this for cab fare, please, and let me know when you need more." I couldn't take the money, of course, but what a jewel she was to offer it.

By the time all the parcels were open, it looked like a gingham cyclone had swept through the room. We played with laying this fabric against that until my stomach reminded me that breakfast had been long, long ago.

I reached for another cookie and pulled my hand back when I realized it was the last. "It's bad luck to take the old maid," I observed.

Ruby sat back. "Oh, you're probably famished!"

I was, but it seemed poor manners to say so. Especially when it was clear she'd had no time to prepare a meal, not with all our fussing over Pearl's quilt.

"I should have told you straight off that there'd been a change of plans." She smoothed a ruffle on the apricot dress. "Mr. Wilkes invited me out to supper. I hope you don't mind."

"No, no. Of course not." I glanced at the mantel clock. "You probably need to get ready." I stood up.

"I'll cook for you next week," she promised, fingering a gold chain at her neck.

"Oh, that reminds me." I picked up a bit of paper that had fallen under the settee. "Is your locket repaired yet?"

She blinked. "Locket?"

I pointed to my own neck. "The one with Pearl's photograph? I'd love to see what she looks like."

"Oh, that locket." She smiled. "No, it wasn't ready. The jeweler was behind." She shrugged. "The holiday and all that. I'm sorry about supper, Hattie."

"Don't give it a thought. But next time, I would love to see your photo albums. Say." I looked at the jumble of dry goods lying about. "Why don't I take some of this and begin cutting out pieces? Pearl will be here before we know it. We'd best get busy on this quilt!"

Monday at eight, I began to get ready for work. As I performed my toilette, I realized that the plus side of keeping night hours was that I had the bathroom all to myself.

I gave my new dress a pat but reached for my second-best shirtwaist and wool skirt, which I'd shortened the night before to a more fashionable six inches from the floor.

Raymond was dozing at the front desk as I tiptoed through the lobby. The cool evening air brushed me with memories of evenings on the prairie enjoying a well-earned rest after a full day.

My footsteps echoed in the quiet streets. I passed a yawning shopkeeper carrying his street-side displays back into his shop, a policeman, and assorted delivery boys. I saw only one or two other women, in sturdy oxfords like my own, no doubt on their way to jobs similar to mine.

The tube lights over the entrance to the Chronicle Building flickered and fluttered like fireflies on a summer night. I rapped on the great glass door. As Miss Tight Corset had promised, the night watchman was there to let me in. Even though I was fairly certain Ned was long gone at this hour, I peered around as I entered. The coast was clear.

The night watchman directed me to the cleaning supply room. There I met some of my coworkers. One was a solid woman with tight curls and tight lips. She gathered her bucket and duster and mop with much thumping and bumping.

"That's Bernice," a girl about my age explained. "And I'm Emmaline McLeary, but they call me Spot."

Her freckled face gave every explanation I might need as to why she was called such. I told her my name. "Welcome," she said. "Up or down?"

Before I could confess that I didn't understand her question, Bernice spoke up. "New girls work down. Them's the rules."

Spot turned to me. "Do you mind, then, Hattie?"

"Oh, you want me to clean downstairs. Sure, I can do that." This was perfect. I'd soon make my way to the morgue sans Ned's help!

"Lunch at two," Bernice grunted. "In there." She jabbed with her chin at a dreary room to my right.

"Is there a place to leave my things?"

Another grunt and jab from Bernice.

"Here, let me show you." Spot led me into the little lunch-room, with its row of cubbies. "That locker's free. Go ahead."

I put my things in the open locker, closed it, turned the key in the lock, and pinned the key to my shirtwaist.

"Percy—he's the night guard—puts coffee on for us at midnight. Long as you get your work done, we don't count the coffee breaks." Spot locked up her pocketbook and hat, handed me a smock embroidered with *San Francisco Chronicle* across the bodice, and dressed herself in matching garb.

I had never thought I would be grateful for my time at Mrs. Brown's boardinghouse, but that was the state in which I found myself as I whipped through the offices on the lower floor. I shared a cup of coffee and conversation with Spot and Bernice during my break but decided I would forgo my wee-hours "lunch" for a respite of a different sort.

When two a.m. rolled around, I found myself in front of a massive wooden door with a faded hand-painted sign that read MORGUE. My emblazoned smock would serve as permission enough, should anyone stop me. But at this hour, it was highly unlikely. Still, I brought my feather duster with me, just in case.

It took both hands to open that door, especially since those hands were trembling. Entering such a dark place, at such a dark hour, was enough to wobble anybody's knees! As I pulled at the handle, a dank and musty perfume wiggled its way out of the opening. I stepped inside, bracing the door with my body as it closed so that it wouldn't slam.

I felt like Alice after she'd fallen down the rabbit hole. To think that all of this was the result of two brothers starting a

82

newspaper with a twenty-dollar loan, way back in 1865. Who was I to dare to pull down one of those weighty, oversized leather-clad volumes and peruse the old issues bound inside? I ran my fingers across a row of bindings, summoning the courage to begin. Sadly, the oldest volumes had been destroyed in the great earthquake and fire of 1906. I shivered a little, to think of this big city in shambles and smoke that April day. Back in Iowa, we worried about tornadoes, not earthquakes. I hoped I never had to experience one. Odd, wasn't it, that both the great earthquake and our great president's assassination had happened in the month of April. And didn't the War Between the States begin and end in that same month? All events years apart, of course, but still. Peculiar coincidence.

Enough woolgathering. There was work to be done. A mystery to solve. I reached for a volume labeled *1915*. Ruby had regaled me with the story of her first meeting with Uncle Chester. "It was springtime," she'd said with a starry look in her eyes. "At the International Exposition. I was touring it with friends. A ruffian stole my pocketbook and Chester chased him down and got it back." She had sighed. "In the end, the only thing stolen that day was my heart."

When she told me that story, I wondered how he could have left if she felt that way about him. I pondered this question for only a moment before my own guilt about Charlie pinched me. Perhaps it was a family trait, to leave the one you loved.

What a sappy train of thought. I sat at the library table, opened the volume, and thumbed through the pages until my eyes watered from the strain. Nothing jumped out at me.

And my lunch break was up. Reluctantly I slid the volume back, making a mental note of which issue to start with when I returned. Because until I found what I was looking for— whatever that was!—I would keep coming back

Two hours later, I had finished cleaning my section and made my way to the break room, glad for the chance to sit down. Bernice wasn't much for anything aside from the occasional grunt, but Spot made up for her lack of conversation. Spot told me about each of her four sisters. "Mabs works at a cigar factory, the twins help Da at the shop, but Tinny, she's the one. A nurse! Registered." Spot shook her head. "She got my share of the family brains and then some, Tinny did." Spot gave herself short shrift. She had brains; a person couldn't spin out stories the way she did without them.

When quitting time rolled around, two thoughts occupied my mind on the walk home: a hot bath and Spot's sisters. All of them working instead of staying at home, a highly unlikely scenario before the war. That was something to think about, wasn't it? To write about? I envisioned a headline, "Women at Work," and articles about different shopgirls and telephone operators and nurses and, yes, even cleaning ladies, throughout the city. That would have a San Francisco hook, wouldn't it?

I reached the Cortez and tugged open the lobby door. But would anyone read such a series? Anyone besides me? "Quit grasping at straws," I scolded myself, not realizing I'd said the words aloud.

"Did you say something, Miss Hattie?" Raymond asked, stashing his bottle under the desk.

I shook my head. "Just mumbling. Any mail?"

"One skinny letter," he said. He held it out to me. It was skinny, all right, but that one letter was worth dozens. It was from Charlie! I read it three times right away, and then again while heating soup on the hot plate.

Dear Hattie,

I had supper again last night with Perilee and Karl. They are good folks, and I can see why they have come to feel like family to you. Perilee said I should write you to tell you my news though I am sure you are too busy with your new life to worry much about what I am up to. Mr. Boeing liked my idea about moving the fuel tanks on his new fighter planes. So I am in charge of making that happen.

Well, I won't take up much more of your time.

Charlie

The letter was short, to be sure, and there was a bit of a cranky tone to it, but I deserved that. It was such a relief to hear from him. I took it as an invitation to write back, to write a real letter, though I'd hold off on telling him about my new job. He might not understand.

That was an odd thought. Ever since we'd met, I could count on Charlie to understand me, even when I didn't myself. I cherished my new friends, but something in me longed for old friends, for friends who knew how I'd gotten the scar on my left knee (shinnying down the Hawley elm tree) or that I had a sweet tooth for lemon drops or that, until Mr.

Whiskers had pussyfooted into my life, I had been afraid of the dark.

Truth be told, it wasn't old friends I missed. It was one old friend.

And whose fault is that, Miss Hattie Brooks? I asked myself.

Setting aside that painful thought, I stitched a bit on Pearl's quilt before crawling under my own for some much-needed sleep.

{ 8 }

Surprises and Cigars

July 14, 1919

Dear Perilee,

Oh, that little dickens, Lottie, already taking her first steps. She's probably itching to keep up with her big brother and sister! I look forward to seeing those photographs of your new house by Green Lake when you can send them. Chase must be in heaven with a fishing hole only blocks away. What a funny story about that old cat stealing one of his fish. Smart cat!

While I don't know when I will make the trip north to see you all, you will be pleased to know about the empty cold cream jar on my dresser, set aside for pennies and dimes for train fare.

You asked about Ruby. She is overjoyed that she'll soon be reunited with Pearl. I cannot wait to meet my little "cousin." I best finish now if I want to get this out in today's mail.

Your friend,
Hattie

I shook the cold cream jar for the comfort of it. Not much of a jingle yet, but every little bit would get me closer to a trip north and a place at Perilee's old oak kitchen table, sipping coffee and eating strudel. I'd jostle Lottie on my lap, read stories to Fern, and maybe even go fishing with Chase. The anticipation of such sweet moments would help keep my pocketbook clasped tight against any nonessentials.

It wasn't all to the bad that I didn't have enough saved up. A trip to Seattle would put me in Charlie's territory. He would not understand my staying in San Francisco to scrub toilets.

Speaking of which, it was time to head to work. It'd only taken a week to get into the rhythm of starting my "day" when most folks were headed to bed and ending it about the time the roosters began to crow back on the homestead. No matter the job, working for a morning newspaper required odd hours. Most reporters, like Ned, showed up at noon, though with Miss D'Lacorte, it was more like one o'clock. They'd work through till nine or ten on a regular basis and sometimes later, their hours dictated by the news itself. The only folks with set start and end times were the night editors and copy readers—they worked six p.m. to two a.m.—and the custodial staff, like Spot, Bernice, and me. The night editor at the *Chronicle* was a man people called Boss Keats; no one seemed to know his real first name. With a nickname like that, you'd think he'd be crustier than a day-old loaf, but he was as gentlemanly as they come. Always asked after my health, if our paths crossed. And took a sincere interest in the answer.

Before I locked the door to my room, I double-checked to make sure the journal Miss Clare had given me was in my pocketbook. I'd decided that it was to be the receptacle for my San Francisco writings and notations. And thanks to Spot and her sisters, I'd filled quite a few pages. I'd even managed to squeeze ten words out of Bernice: "Anybody can scrub a floor. But I can make it shine." My idea had jelled. I would write a series called *Female 49ers: San Francisco Women Who Find Gold in Their Work.* Not that anyone wanted it, mind you, but believing is the first rung up any dream's ladder. I figured if I enjoyed the stories I was gathering, others would, too.

Bernice and Spot were good sorts but the sorts others seemed to ignore. In fact, in our blue smocks, we were all virtually invisible, except to Boss Keats. Even Miss Tight Corset had given me a blank stare when I'd smiled at her early one morning. I doubted that it had ever occurred to people like her or Ned or even Miss D'Lacorte that the women wearing the navy blue smocks had lives—and hopes!—of their own. That was why I kept plugging away on my stories. Plus, I was pigheaded enough to think that the newspapers could print another point of view about women in the work world. Since the war had ended, most men thought working gals should hang up their hats and tools and head back to the kitchen.

My showing an interest in Spot's sisters had softened Bernice's sharp ways; even so, I was not prepared for her suggestion that night.

"You take the newsroom floor," she said as she buttoned on her smock.

"But I thought new girls start down." I repeated her edict from my first night on the job.

"Things can change," she said. And that was that. Spot winked at me and crossed her fingers for luck. I'd spilled my dream to them the second day we'd worked together. Perhaps they thought that my mere presence on that very floor would transform me into a reporter. I had to chuckle at that, but their belief in me put wings on my feet, and on my heart.

"Oh, no." I froze in my tracks. "What about Ned?"

They knew about him as well, and that he was not yet aware that I was already employed at the *Chronicle*. I'd made Maude promise not to tell.

"I'll go up first," offered Spot. "If the coast is clear, I'll give you a signal." She hooted three times. "Like this."

I grinned. "The perfect warning for us night owls."

We rode the elevator together but I exited one floor ahead of her. The plan was that I'd listen in the stairwell for her all clear.

I felt like Nellie Bly on secret assignment when I heard the trio of hoots. I thanked Spot as we passed on the stairs.

At midnight, I caught up with my colleagues in the break room.

"Well," Spot asked, pouring me a cup of coffee. "Anything to report?"

I took it from her. "Only that someone must have had a sauerkraut sandwich for lunch yesterday." I pinched my nose. "The whole newsroom reeked."

"Bunch of slobs," Bernice observed with a nod.

That was Spot's cue to fill us in on Tinny's new beau, who was as slovenly as Tinny was neat. My mind drifted a bit, as this was a topic Spot had visited before. The newsroom folks might be a bunch of slobs, but what I wouldn't give to be one of them!

We polished off the molasses cookies Bernice had brought in to share and got back to work, with Bernice and Spot heading up and me down. They loved cleaning in the composing room, with all those great huge machines. I was delighted to work where I could more easily make my way to the morgue.

When my two a.m. lunch break rolled around, I quickly ate my bologna sandwich, then skipped down another flight and pulled open that heavy door to history. First impressions might lead one to think that a newspaper morgue was as quiet as . . . well, as a morgue. Not that I knew about *that* firsthand. But I did not think of "my" morgue as quiet. Even in the wee hours, a symphony of sounds reverberated throughout this place. First heard was the *thwup* as one weighty volume was slid from its shelf, followed by the satisfying *thump* as it was placed on the library table. Then the *whisk-whisk* refrain of pages being turned enhanced the concerto. One last set of sounds rounded out the music of a city's memories: each time

I delved into those huge leather books, each time I traced my finger over the yellowed columns of newsprint, each time I studied a worn and faded photograph, papery whispers spoke to me of things that had happened long ago, and in so many places it would take an entire atlas to contain them all. These stories of real people were as irresistible to me as the Italian nougats one of Maude's suitors had brought her.

Flipping through old newsprint was a bit like attending church services. Aunt Ivy would be horrified if she ever heard me compare the two—one focused on man and one on God—but I had come to believe that there was something sacred in telling stories and telling them true. I smoothed the page on the table in front of me. One day, I would create stories like those printed here. I knew it.

But when I looked at the many volumes yet on the shelves, my task seemed akin to finding a needle in a stack of hay. All those pages! It was deflating to consider perusing each sheet of each issue from 1915 on, in order to find one tiny key, however rusty, to my uncle's past. If I had been back in Arlington, it would have been a snap. In a small town, everyone ends up in the paper at some time or another, and not just in the birth announcements or obituaries. A ladies' luncheon would earn many column inches. New hymnals at the Baptist church would rate a headline in bold. And a farmer's just-delivered tractor would make front-page news.

In a city as big as San Francisco, a person could evidently drift through, silent and stealthy, and evaporate without a trace, like the familiar fog under the strength of the sun.

With a sigh, I flopped open the volume for 1915 to July 1,

to pick up where I'd left off. I read through my lunch hour, barely scratching the surface, then pushed back in my chair, rubbing my eyes from the strain. It was no use! I'd never find anything. Never come up with that story that would truly hook Mr. Monson's attention and hook me a newspaper job. I was about to turn the page when something jumped out at me. Under an article about a woman who'd been passing counterfeit traveler's checks was a column titled "In the Hotels." I'd noticed this particular column before. But here was a name I recognized: Chester Hubert Wright.

A thrill zinged through me as I scanned the line. Uncle Chester! Registered at the Hotel Sutter. Did this notice mean he'd recently arrived? Or had he been in town awhile? I began flipping backward through earlier issues. His name had appeared the week before. And the week before that. I kept flipping. The earliest date he was listed was Wednesday, May 12. That fit with Ruby's memory that they'd met in the spring. I pulled out my notebook and wrote down the hotel's name, making a mental note to look up the address later. I closed the big book, giving the front cover a pat. Well-begun was half done!

The nights at work soon fell into a similar routine—I'd start in the newsroom and migrate to the morgue, trying to peel my uncle's story from those yellowed pages. Aside from learning that he'd roomed at the Sutter, I hadn't made much progress. But I was getting quite the education about this town around the time of the Panama Pacific International Exposition. San Francisco had been determined to show it had completely recovered from the earthquake, and the exposition was just the ticket for proving that. The marvel drew visitors by the thousands, including the famous, like Helen Keller, flying ace Eddie Rickenbacker, and Charlie Chaplin. Henry Ford's onsite assembly plant turned out one automobile every ten minutes for three hours each afternoon. Imagine that! But the spectacle also attracted the infamous, including one enterprising duo selling imitations of the Novagems that glittered from the exposition's Tower of Jewels. The Tower's jewels *were* sold, but not until after the fair closed in December. This pair of confidence artists jumped the gun by several months. "We'll catch them," then Sheriff Thomas A. Finn promised in a headline. But further research uncovered no evidence of that promise fulfilled. It seemed the fair "exposed" the worst of humankind as well as the best. No matter—the more I read, the more I wished I could have seen such sights for myself. It was incredible to think that nothing from the fair had been built to last; the only token of its existence now was the Palace of Fine Arts on the Presidio grounds.

During our coffee break, I asked Bernice and Spot if they'd visited the exposition.

"Once." Spot sighed. "It was amazing! I caught a glimpse of Thomas Edison!"

"It was a lot of fuss over nothing," Bernice grumbled. "I had better uses for fifty cents!"

Spot's eyes glittered. "But for that fifty-cent admission, I have fifty dollars' worth of memories."

"Huh," Bernice grunted. She finished her coffee. "Back to work."

I didn't know what would impress Bernice, if an exposition that lured the world to San Francisco's doorstep had failed to. She reminded me of my early efforts at bread-baking on the homestead, with crusts as hard as stone over a slightly spongy center. If she were hard through and through, she never would've given me a chance to clean the newsroom. And I never would have found what I did, a few days later, as I was dusting. It was only a piece of scrap paper on a desktop, but scribbled across it was a question—"date of Tetrazzini free concert? Christmas . . .'09? '10? Check the morgue."

It was as if the message had been left for me. I pulled my notebook out of my apron pocket, tore out a page, and copied the message down carefully. Instead of joining Bernice and Spot for coffee, I slipped down to the morgue and pulled down the volume holding the December 1910 issues.

Bingo! There it was. "Two Hundred and Fifty Thousand Hear Tetrazzini Sing in the Open Air Before the Chronicle Building." I got shivers looking at the photo of the streets outside the very building I was cleaning, streets teeming with people as far as you could see. Imagine it! Skimming the article, I smiled at some of the flowery description of the audience: "a monumental microcosm of humanity itself . . . bootblacks rubbed elbows with bankers and painted creatures with fat and wholesome mothers of families." But still, I could forgive the writer. It must have been some evening. I scribbled "December 24, 1910" on the page from my notebook, put the journal back on the shelf, and hurried upstairs, where I tucked my answer under the carriage bar on the typewriter on the desk, third from the back on the far left. The desk where I'd found the scrap of paper.

Then I scurried back downstairs and back to work, a bit

disappointed I wouldn't see the look on the reporter's face when he discovered an answer to his question. I felt like one of the shoemaker's elves, and that made me almost giddy. Tracking down that date had been as satisfying as pounding a fencepost nail in straight and true. And a lot less strenuous. I started to hum a song that Maude often sang, "A Little Bit of Heaven." My good-deed caper felt like a little bit of heaven. I sighed. A little bit of what it might be like to work as a reporter.

The next evening, the newsroom was abuzz, so I altered my routine and began on a different floor. I had just fetched a fresh bucket of soapy water when I heard my name.

"Hattie?" Bernice's voice carried down the long hall to where I was cleaning. I poked my head out of the room. "Yes?"

"Best come out here." The tone of her voice made me want to do just the opposite. But Bernice was not the sort to be ignored. I stepped into the hall.

And came face to face with Ned, as well as a potbellied man who stood behind him, unlit cigar clenched in his teeth.

"Hattie?" Ned stared at me.

"Ned." I forced a smile. "You're working late."

"Several of us are. But that's neither here nor there. What are you doing?"

I wanted nothing more than to hide behind the feather duster in my hand. Instead I waggled it. "Cleaning."

"Cleaning?" He couldn't have looked more surprised if I'd told him I was planning a bank robbery.

"I guess I should have mentioned it." I noticed a picture frame on the wall and swished the feather duster over it.

"Well. Yes. Cleaning." He blinked, then shook his head as if to clear it. "Nothing wrong with that, but"—he waved the piece of paper I'd left under the typewriter—"I think you could be doing something different." He turned and pointed to the man behind him. "Which is what I was explaining to Mr. Monson here."

Mr. Monson! The managing editor.

"How do you do, sir?" I tucked the feather duster behind my back.

Mr. Monson switched the cigar to the other side of his mouth. "Terrible. My ulcer's acting up and Kirk here is about to give me a migraine with another addlepated idea."

I smiled meekly.

"Here's what I was thinking." Ned stroked his moustache. "No reporter I know likes to waste time in the morgue. Not when there are hot stories to track down."

Mr. Monson chomped.

"So I suggested that we hire you. Like a stringer. Only instead of reporting, you'd research."

"No reporting?" I said.

"At least, not right away," Ned added hastily.

"Not likely ever," groused Mr. Monson.

Bernice grunted and he backed up two paces. "Well—"

"One step at a time," Ned said brightly. "Now, come on, Hattie, and let's discuss your new position."

I couldn't leave Bernice and Spot in the lurch. "My day ends at six."

Mr. Monson squawked. "I'll be sawing logs by then."

"What about if I come in to work a little early tomorrow night? Say nine? Could we talk then?"

Again Mr. Monson's cigar switched sides. He squinted at me, but then he nodded. "We could," he said.

And with that, they were gone.

I couldn't help myself. I gave Bernice a huge hug. "You are my fairy godmother," I told her.

She eased out of my clutches. "Pshaw. It's all your doing, Hattie." Then she did something so un-Bernice-like, I nearly fainted. She smiled. "You show 'em," she said. "For us."

The next night, exactly at nine p.m., I made my way to the newsroom. Ned was watching for me and waved when I stepped off the elevator. The hangers-on by the door parted like the Red Sea as I made my way into the lion's den. Or, to be precise, the Tiger Woman's den!

Ned escorted me into Mr. Monson's office and within five minutes I was being escorted back out, with a new job. Two days a week, I would come to the newsroom around eight to see if I had a research assignment. If there wasn't one, I could do some filing instead, or make myself useful, in Mr. Monson's words, before starting my cleaning shift. And they'd pay me a dollar a week!

"Never heard of such a thing before," Mr. Monson had grumbled. "But I'll give it a two-week trial. Got it?"

I had nodded, then stuck out my hand. Again I was subjected to his squint, but he stuck out his hand, too, and I shook with the firm grip of one who'd set nearly five hundred rods of fence. I thought I saw a look of approval on his face. But then again, it could've been indigestion. "Shall I start tomorrow?" I asked.

"Fine." With that, he had shooed us out of his office.

At the elevator, I grabbed Ned's hands. "Thank you, thank you!"

"I didn't do anything," he said. "But you can count on me to spread the word around the office. Though, if you want to feel indebted to me, I don't mind." He pressed my hands before letting go. "In fact, I rather like it, Hattie."

He said the words as if they were arrows and he were Cupid zinging them into my heart.

The elevator arrived and I practically leaped in. "See you later." Thankfully, the doors closed quickly. I leaned against the brass rail. What was that about? Men!

"Watch that you don't scour the paint right off that wall," Bernice scolded moments later as I got to work.

"Sorry." I eased up on the scrub brush. "I guess I'm just excited about the new job." No sense mentioning Ned's craziness to her. The shift passed quickly and I was soon on my way back to the hotel.

Raymond handed me a message when I entered the lobby. It was from Ruby. "Please call" was all it said. He patiently allowed me to dial yet one more free call.

"Hattie?" Her voice escaped in a little sob. "It's Pearl. She's sick."

"I'll be right over," I told her.

When I arrived, Ruby was limp on the settee. "I'm so worried," she said. I brought a cool cloth to wash her face and then went straight to the kitchen to make her a cup of tea.

She managed to sit up and take it from me. The trembling in her hands seemed to ease as she sipped. "I've got to go to her."

"Of course you do." I could only imagine how desperate she must feel now, so far from her little girl. "And don't worry about Mr. Wilkes. I'm sure he'll understand."

She set her teacup down. "You are so good to me. I am mortally embarrassed to have to ask this. But there was a problem at my bank. . . ." Her voice trailed off. "I don't quite have enough for the train ticket."

"How much do you need?" I reached for my pocketbook.

She named the amount. It was a goodly sum. Everything I had in my pocketbook, in fact.

What was I thinking? I hadn't been able to help our little Mattie, in the end. But here was the chance to help another sick little girl. And didn't I have two jobs now?

I put the money on the table. Ruby took my hands and squeezed them hard. "I'll send word as soon as I know anything."

"She'll be fine," I said, squeezing back. "She'll be just fine."

That night, I prayed fervently that my assurances to Ruby would come true.

❧ 9 ❧

Home Runs and Inches

July 29, 1919

Dear Leafie,

I write you because I could not worry Perilee with news of a sick child. Ruby's little Pearl took ill a week or so ago. I wish you'd been there in Santa Clara with your black bag of potions. You would've known what to give her to get her back in the pink. Ruby has reported that some small improvement was noted yesterday, for which I am very grateful. Such glad tidings help me walk with a lighter step.

While the elevator rattled upward, I reflected on what I'd learned from Ruby that morning. Pearl had turned a corner, so plans were once again being set in motion to bring her to San Francisco. I was now even more eager to meet my young cousin.

In a sunnier frame of mind than I'd had in days, I stepped out into the newsroom, searching for Ace McCovey, sporting writer for the *Chronicle*. One of the office boys had found me downstairs the day before to report that Ace needed help with a baseball history question. Though it was to be my day off, I'd said yes. One thing I'd quickly learned was that there are no regular hours for reporters. No time like the present to get used to that notion. My two-week probation was nearly up. And every reporter I'd done research for had been pleased with my efforts. Ned was so certain Mr. Monson would continue the arrangement that he was hosting a dinner for me with Maude and her new beau to mark the occasion. But I'd hung around long enough now to know that it might please Mr. Monson to give me the boot simply because that was what the reporters *didn't* want.

I paused a moment, on the edges of the newsroom. That anyone got any work done with all this noise and commotion was nothing short of miraculous. How I loved my small role in this miracle! I fervently believed that one day I would have a larger role. I might never be a Nellie Bly, but wouldn't it be better to be Hattie Brooks? In daydreams, my writing life was replete with glories.

"Daydreams" was the word for it. I'd already ascertained the kinds of stories a young woman reporter would likely be assigned: "Get a Turban—Don't Be Dowdy," or "The Monocle: Fashion Fad?" or "A French Theme Is Planned for Mrs. So-and-So's Annual Luncheon."

I made my way to Ace's desk, where he was engrossed in a heated conversation with Mr. Monson. Ace jabbed his thick index finger on a page of the editor's open assignment book. "You've got me working double duty. I can't cover the Seals *and* the auto race!"

"Well, you're the sporting news. Who else should do it?" Mr. Monson switched his damp cigar to the other side of his mouth. "If you don't want this job, I can hire someone else."

Ace loosened his loud tie, answering Mr. Monson's threat at length, with a few colorful expressions thrown in for good measure. If Aunt Ivy'd been in the vicinity, there would have been a bar of soap applied to Ace's mouth. With vigor.

"Oh, for crying out loud." He swabbed his forehead with a bandanna handkerchief the size of North Dakota. "I didn't see you there, Hattie. Sorry about the language."

I'd heard worse in the newsroom. "No offense taken. Did you have something for me?"

He nodded, pawing around on his messy desk until he found the proper scrap of paper. As I walked away with it, he and Mr. Monson resumed their "discussion." Each appeared determined to win the argument by sheer volume alone.

"I have a solution for you," Ned called when they both stopped to take a breath.

"What?" Mr. Monson snarled.

"*Who*," Ned replied.

The cigar switched sides again. "Don't get smart with me, buster."

"Heaven forbid I should do that!" Ned pushed back from his desk. "What I meant was that my solution is a who."

"Who?" Ace and Mr. Monson echoed together.

Ned pointed. "Her."

Two heads pivoted as one, eyes looking first at Ned and then at me.

"Har-di-har-har," Mr. Monson said in a flat voice. "Very funny." He slapped the assignment book shut.

A buzz erupted from the crew by the elevators. "I'll cover it," some brave soul called out.

Ace tapped some notes I'd given him last week against his desktop. "She's got a way with words," he said. "I can vouch for that."

Mr. Monson chomped hard on his cigar. "I am not running a kindygarten here!" he blustered. "And what in tarnation does she know about baseball?"

Heaven only knows what possessed me. Maybe the good report about Pearl made me think anything was possible. Maybe it was Ned's taking up my cause. Or maybe it was like Aunt Ivy said: "Fools rush in where angels fear to tread."

"I know a goodly amount," I said, clear and strong. "Not only that, I am a fairly respectable pitcher." That was thanks to Charlie, who'd taken it upon himself to teach me, a southpaw, to throw the ball.

"Oh, my ulcer." Mr. Monson grabbed his middle. "Get my Bromo-Seltzer!"

"Stupendous idea." Gill, the police beat man, slapped his hands together. "I can't wait to read the little lady's breathless prose. 'Oh, it was so much fun to watch those nice men run all around those darling little bases,'" he intoned in a falsetto.

"Don't you think she can do it?" Miss D'Lacorte asked, her tone a dare and a vote of confidence all in one. This was the closest I'd come yet to her actually speaking to me.

"She's a kid!" Gill sputtered. "Okay, maybe she can write a sentence or two, but it takes skill to cover sports."

"That doesn't seem to stop Ace," someone called out, and the room bubbled with laughter. Even Ace joined in.

"Mr. Monson, if I strike Gill out, will you give me the game assignment?" The question slid out of my mouth, completely bypassing the common sense part of my brain.

He rubbed his hand over his mouth, forgetting about the cigar. He barely managed to catch it before it went flying. "Out of the question!"

"Where would we get the equipment?" one of the hangers-on shouted. The gaggle of them had crept away from their usual spot by the elevator, venturing into heretofore forbidden territory. One particularly bold hopeful now leaned against Ned's desk.

Ace jerked open a desk drawer and called out, "Play ball!"

Gill ducked as the ball bolted toward us. I snagged it. Left-handed.

Mr. Monson's cigar waggled.

"What will I use for a bat?" Gill was beginning to sound like a whiny schoolboy.

The words were no sooner out of his mouth before office boys began scouring the premises. They not only came up with a bat—left over from the last newsboys' picnic—but with a right-handed glove. "You're a southpaw like me," said the elevator boy. He told me that he stored his glove in his work locker to keep it out of reach of a sticky-fingered younger brother. "But I'd be glad for you to use it."

"Looks like we've got all the necessary equipment," said Ace.

"This is nonsense." Gill slumped lower in his desk chair.

Someone clucked like a chicken.

"If you're afraid . . . ," Ace started.

Gill glowered at him. "Let's get it over with."

Flash Finnegan followed us out the door.

"No cameras!" Gill blocked his way.

Flash pointed to the Graflex around his neck. "Camera," he said, emphasizing the *a* at the end of the word. "Singular."

Gill's growl caused Flash to cackle gleefully. "On our way, then, men!" Flash called. "Oh, I should say, men and lady." He bowed deeply to me, bracing his precious camera against his chest. We were quite the parade, winding through the composing room and down several flights of stairs to the dingy metal doors on the backside of the building. Out in the alley, Ace threw down a copy of yesterday's front page to stand in for home plate and then paced off the distance to my pitcher's mound, which was last Sunday's funnies.

"This okay, Hattie?" Ace asked.

I nodded.

"Do you want to warm up?" He pounded his left palm with his right fist.

It seemed a long way to home plate. Farther than I was used to. But I knew he was being fair. I shook my head.

Flash hooted. "That's crust for you!"

It was then I noticed that Mr. Monson had followed us outside as well. In fact, he was carrying the newsboys' bat. He presented it to Gill. "Play ball!"

Without any discussion, Ace stepped in as umpire. My

new friend, the elevator boy, squatted in front of him, playing catcher.

The first thing I did was unbutton the sleeves on my shirtwaist and roll them up. Ladies' clothes are not designed for baseball. Then I put my foot on the funnies, smack dab on Mutt and Jeff. I took a deep breath, reminding myself of what Charlie had taught me. "The first rule in pitching," he always said, "is never to aim the ball."

Down the alley, Gill jabbed at the air with a few powerful practice swings. I imagine his goal was to intimidate, but he was accomplishing quite the opposite. His performance was akin to sending a telegraph from Western Union. Watching him, I was betting that he'd go after the high heat. I decided to save my specialty, the snake ball, to use only if needed. Well, and maybe to show off a little. I hid a grin behind my borrowed glove.

Even though my body was in a narrow San Francisco alley, my head was back in Iowa, on one of the sweetest fields ever, at the back of the Hawley barn, where Charlie had painted a target. Those had been sunshine days, all glow and easiness, without one care in the world. When Charlie had been my pitching coach and nothing more.

I couldn't afford such distracting thoughts right now. I had a batter to face down.

As if it were just me and Charlie, behind their barn, I went through my motion and released the ball.

"Strike one!" Ace called.

"Lucky break." Gill tapped the bat against his shoe. "Watch out," he taunted. "This one's going for Oakland!"

Another deep breath and another release. Not as smooth, but it did the trick.

"Stee-rike two."

Gill dropped his bat and glared at Ace. "That was no strike!"

Ace folded his beefy arms across his chest. "I calls 'em as I sees 'em." He motioned for Gill to turn around and stand up to the plate.

I wasn't one to brag. I was a good pitcher. But games we played back home weren't regulation. This was the first time I'd ever had to propel a ball sixty feet. My shoulder ached. And it showed.

"Ball one!" Ace called it fairly. I'd known it was a ball as soon as it left my hand. The next two pitches were ball two and ball three.

"Full count," someone murmured, as if I didn't know. Full count. I was in a heap of trouble with one last chance to strike Gill out. I could almost hear Aunt Ivy sniping: "Pride goeth before a fall." Was it prideful to believe I could do a good job with that baseball game assignment? No. But claiming that I could strike Gill out *was* purely prideful. And purely foolish. I thought back to a similar situation at that one Fourth of July picnic. My confidence—no, my pride—had landed me in the same kind of predicament. And in that instance, the batter had won the day. Then it had been for fun; this time a part of my dream was at stake.

Well, nothing ventured, nothing gained. If I didn't manage to throw a strike with this last pitch, I would at the very least give my ragtag audience a good show. The snake ball was my own little invention. Charlie couldn't hit it. Most of the time. If this had been a real game, any sensible catcher would've called me off this decision. But there was no sensible catcher, only an elevator boy. And my own fool self.

Here is what I did: shifted the ball so that the seams rested crossways against my fingers. Rolled back my shoulders and took a deep breath. Cast a hard look in Gill's direction. Then I let the ball fly. It slithered out of my hand and hissed through the air.

Gill never saw it.

"Strike three!" Ace clapped his leg. "If that don't beat all!"

There were a few cheers for me and a few slaps on Gill's back. He walked out to the "mound" and stuck out his hand. "I can't say I enjoyed having a girl strike me out, but well done."

I toned my grin down to a modest smile and shook. "You're a good sport, Gill," I told him. The elevator boy reclaimed his precious glove and the crowd dispersed. I'd worked up some heat with the exercise. Even though it might be true that "horses sweat, men perspire, but ladies merely glow," I'd gone well beyond glowing. I fanned myself and moved inside to get a drink of water.

Mr. Monson caught me on my way to the ladies' room. "I guess you have yourself an assignment," he said. "Earned fair and square."

"Thank you, sir." Ace dropped two Seals tickets in my hand. I knew exactly who I'd ask to be my companion. I owed it to him. Even though Ned insisted on buying the peanuts and soda, we had a wonderful afternoon. I felt quite the real reporter with my notepad propped on my knees, taking notes. It turns out that Ned was no baseball fan, but I assured him I wouldn't hold it against him. Much.

• • •

The San Francisco Nine Rout Portland

By DORA DEAN

Baseball is a true equalizer of men. Where else does the banker share a wooden bleacher with a newsboy, a preacher with a police officer, a lawyer with a longshoreman? And where else but at the new Old Rec Park can Dora Dean and her fellow females be accepted as one of the crowd?

Maude stopped reading aloud, marking her place with a finger. "You're going to need to start a scrapbook. Ned says this is four whole column inches. Not bad for a novice!"

"Notice that it's hidden on the last page of the sporting section."

"Last page is better than no page at all," she scolded.

"Agreed." Though I'd done my best to persuade Mr. Monson to let me use my own name, he'd saddled me with the Dora Dean byline, a nom de plume shared by any number of *Chronicle* women reporters. I took the clipping from Maude. My words in print! It was a thrill, byline or no. I had miles to go before I earned the right to use my own name, like Miss D'Lacorte. But look at that! Four column inches! I was moving up in the newspaper world.

August 4, 1919

Dear Charlie,

I'm not surprised that Mr. Boeing and his friend Mr. Hubbard are impressed with your work. This first promotion of yours will not be your last, I would imagine.

Enclosed please find a clipping of my very first article in the Chronicle. *Every female must pay her dues as Dora Dean or Helen White or some such. Next time, I'll get my own byline! Regardless, I wanted you to have a copy of this story, as it was thanks to you that I got to write it.*

Your southpaw snake baller,
Hattie

❧ 10 ❧

A Bird in the Hand

August 17, 1919

Dear Charlie,

Happy birthday! You are an old man of twenty now. Imagine that!

I am in good spirits on your special day. Yesterday, Ruby and I saw the new Charlie Chaplin film. It was wonderful to hear her laugh. Plans remain in place for Pearl to come here, but the doctor advises against travel just yet. Last night, Mr. Wilkes invited me to join him and Ruby for supper at Bernstein's Marine Grotto. Let me say with complete confidence that there will be no more oysters in my future! They must be an acquired taste, for Mr. Wilkes enjoyed a large platter of them.

My series on Spot and her sisters has grown to include some other working girls, most introduced to me by the loquacious Spot. I had not thought about this home-front impact of the war before. It turns out that many women who joined the work world while all the men were away fighting prefer to remain. One of my favorite interviewees was Miss Katherine Rick, who works at the San Francisco Hat Company. I'd never given much thought to men's hats before chatting with her. Her passion for her work is fairly contagious. Sadly, I am doubtful that any but my close circle of friends will ever read this piece. But hope is a thing with feathers, isn't it?

Speaking of which, I've accumulated quite the collection. Of course, Aunt Ivy would say, "Feathers don't make a bird." That may be so, but each time I find one, it feels as if my truest dreams are closer to having wings.

I'd best sign off. I couldn't let this day pass without letting you know I was thinking of you.

Yours,
Hattie

My spirits were as fine as the August weather. Charlie had sent me two letters since I'd written him about the baseball game; we were back on a friendly track, and now I had a day all to myself.

Not that I was complaining, but Ruby and I had been constant companions, holding cozy quilting bees for two at her apartment since her return from Santa Clara. We'd made great progress on Pearl's quilt; the top was nearly all pieced.

113

Ruby had cooked me several meals, and once sent me off to work with a batch of oatmeal raisin cookies to share with Bernice and Spot. I made a point of being available whenever she asked, as I knew my company helped divert her attention from the hole created by Pearl's absence. Even Mr. Wilkes, the kind soul, was doing his best to distract her. They had dined together a handful of times in the past two weeks.

My dance card for the day was completely empty, and that suited me fine. There was some washing and correspondence to catch up on, and my daily reading of the paper from cover to cover as part of my self-taught journalism course, but what I was most looking forward to was finishing my working women series.

After a hot-plate lunch of soup and crackers, I flipped open the journal Miss Clare had given me, tapping pencil against the page as I reread the opening sentence. It was giving me fits. "Among the various forms of employment that enlist the activity of San Francisco's young women, Miss Katherine Ricks believes that few are more fascinating than that to which she gives her attention." A reporter lived and died by the lead and the one I'd written was as lively as liverwurst.

What had I been thinking? I munched another cracker. Maybe the problem was that I was trying to write like some big shot instead of writing like plain old Hattie Brooks. I threw myself forward, head on the desk. My brain was as dry as a summer field. A few taps of my noggin on the hard surface did nothing to shake loose any ideas.

It had never been this difficult to write my Honyocker's Homilies. Maybe it was because they'd started out as letters to Uncle Holt; I'd had no idea he would pass them on to his friend Mr. Miltenberger, the editor of the *Arlington News*. When I'd written them, it was as if we'd been sitting on the front porch of an evening, chatting about the day's events. Maybe I should try to imagine writing this article for Uncle Holt. Or Perilee. Or Charlie.

I pushed myself upright and drew a thick black line through that awful sentence. How would I explain what I'd learned from Spot's sisters and their friends? I shifted my gaze around my room, desperately seeking inspiration. My eyes stopped at my desktop feather bouquet, and I thought about the birds to whom these had once belonged. They never fretted. They simply spread their wings and soared. Why couldn't my words do that as well?

Wait. Spreading one's wings. That was the gist of the stories I'd heard. Some of those girls hadn't even wanted to work initially, but had done so out of patriotic feelings, for the war effort. But once they'd gone to work, they'd found they rather liked it. And now that the war was over, a choir of male voices clamored against them, saying that what they were doing wasn't right.

I picked up my pen and scribbled down the sentence that popped into my brain. "Miss Tinny McLeary sought her starched nurse's cap and uniform out of patriotic duty, but taking it from her now that the war is over would be akin to clipping the wings of a free-flying osprey."

A shiver of pleasure wriggled down my spine as I inked in the period of that sentence. Now, this was a lead I could feel proud of. Of course, revising the lead meant revising the rest of the article. But the time flew by as I scratched words out here and inserted phrases there. I do believe the building could have fallen down right around me and I would not have noticed. It was me and the page and nothing else. No wonder Ned loved his job so! This pushing and pulling at words was exhilarating. I sat back, rereading my efforts. In this moment, it didn't matter that no other eyes might see what I'd written. It felt that good simply to have composed something fine. A story worthy of its subjects.

An idea tapped at the back of my brain. Mr. Monson had given me an old typewriter to use for my baseball story, the one on the desk in the back corner. The *h* key didn't work and the carriage return was stiff, but being as I was a hunt-and-peck typist, it suited me fine. I would type up a copy of my article for each of the girls I'd interviewed. A small token of goodwill for their time. I'd start on it after my shift on Monday.

Someone rapped at my door. *Dum da-da dum dum, dum dum.* That was Maude's "shave and a haircut" knock. I opened the door.

"It's too lovely to stay inside." Maude was dressed in white eyelet, with matching parasol. She looked like a vanilla ice cream cone.

"I have some washing out to do," I told her.

"Nonsense." She grabbed my hand. "The Ocean Boulevard calls," she pronounced. "And there are two very dashing young fellows eager to be our escorts."

"Two?" I asked. I was certain that one was Maude's new beau, Orson.

"Questions later."

"At least let me get my hat." I selected my old hat, not as chic as my cloche but with a wider brim against the sun and salt air.

As promised, there were two young men awaiting us in the lobby. Orson, as I had guessed, and Ned.

"Miss Brooks." Ned tipped his hat to me. "You are a sight for sore eyes."

I made a face. "More like a sore sight." Even if Maude and I exchanged outfits, she would outshine me.

"Tut, tut." Ned wagged his finger. "Here is how a lady accepts a compliment: she says thank you."

"Thank you," I said, adding, "but I don't know about the lady part."

"She's hopeless," Ned said to his sister.

"But that's why you are so mad for her," Maude teased. At least, I hoped it was a tease.

Orson was the proud owner of a brand-new Nash Touring Car, so we hopped in for the ride. He was soon expertly parking it in front of Benson's Pool Hall, in a great row of other automobiles. Ned offered his hand to help me out of the car, but I stopped mid-exit. "Oh, smell that!" I wasn't sure I would ever get enough of that briny air, scented with fish and seaweed and adventure. I turned to Maude. "This was a wonderful idea. Thank you."

She winked. "Thank Ned." Then she grabbed Orson's arm. "Buy me an ice cream," she said, and off they went.

"Do you care for anything, Hattie?" Ned asked.

I shook my head. "Just a walk. It's so glorious." We began

to stroll the boulevard adjacent to the beach. "You'll laugh, but before I'd seen the ocean, I thought it must look like a flax field in bloom." I looked off across the dunes to the sea. "They're not at all alike. Both beautiful, of course. But not alike."

"Do you miss it?" Ned asked. "Do you want to return?"

"To Vida?" I brushed a stray strand of hair from my cheek. It was an interesting question Ned posed. Did I? "To see the people, yes. The place, no." It seemed I'd made a choice not only to move westward, but also to move forward, not back.

"What about Iowa?" He tugged my arm to call my attention to a man in a wool swimming costume doing a handstand on the beach.

I pointed at the reason for the handstand. A threesome of giggling girls. Ned nodded. "So, Iowa?"

"No again." Even when Charlie had still been there, I'd felt no tug to Arlington, or any other part of Iowa.

"Then I stand a chance."

"Come again?" I had to quickstep to avoid a collision with an ice-cream-sticky little boy.

"Never mind." Ned eyed the little boy's ice cream. "That looks good. Are you sure you don't want one?"

"It has gotten a little warm." Even from under my wide-brimmed hat, I was beginning to wilt a bit from the sun.

We made our way to the nearest ice cream stand. I ordered strawberry, Ned chocolate. "This is refreshing. Thank you." I nibbled a bit of fresh berry as we continued our walk past the amusements. A barker called out, "Three tries for a dime. Only one thin dime!" Ned and I wound our way through the crowds of promenaders, proud papas pushing baby buggies, little boys rolling hoops, little girls roller-skating. There were the daring, dressed in swim costumes, and the hangers-on, egging the former to dive into the sea. Enterprising sorts sold all manner of geegaws from wood crate storefronts. I was tempted by a thimble embossed with seals and bought it as a gift for Perilee. I also bought a penny post card of the Great Beach Highway itself.

Above all the people noise, gulls and other seabirds made it clear that this was their domain and we humans mere trespassers.

I chuckled.

"What's so funny?" Ned asked.

"Oh, I was just thinking back on my first day in town. I felt like such a country mouse." I waved with my ice cream cone. "All these people! The noise! The commotion! It gave me the jitters. And now, after a couple of months, it seems normal."

"I'm glad you like it," Ned said. "Because I have a secret plan for keeping you here." He waggled his eyebrows like a mad scientist.

"Oh, dear!" I pressed the back of my hand to my forehead like the women always did in melodramas. "Whatever shall I do?"

He pretended to twist a long moustache. "Say yes." Beneath the silliness, I sensed something else going on. I wasn't sure what it was though.

"To what?" I concentrated on my ice cream cone.

"Being my partner."

"In what?" I asked in a teasing tone. "Crime?"

"In news."

That stopped me in my tracks. "What do you mean?"

He led me over to a bench and we sat. "President Wilson's going to pay a visit to our fair city next month. Trying to get backing for the League of Nations."

"I'd heard that." What I knew about the League of Nations would fit in that thimble I'd bought Perilee.

"So that gives us about two weeks to earn the assignment. There's a lot of background to fill in, to understand."

"You want me to help with the research?" I'd gotten pretty good at that, if I did say so myself.

"That's the ticket." He sat back on the bench. "But I'd pay you myself. Monson doesn't need to know about it. It'd be our little project."

I thought it over. It was flattering that Ned wanted my help. But I knew he aspired to being more than a cub reporter. And something like this could boost his standing. Considerably. I sensed this was the time for some horse-trading. "I'll do it. And you don't have to pay me." I held up my hand to stop his protest. "At least, not in cold hard cash. What I want is the chance to do some of the writing. If it's not up to snuff, you don't have to use it. But if it's newsworthy, you do."

"I've no complaints about your writing." He chewed on my suggestion for a moment. "Seems fair."

"I'm not finished." This might be the chance to hang up my navy blue work smock for good. "We share a byline."

"What?" Ned nearly jumped off the bench. "That's just not done, Hattie."

I shrugged. "Fine." I stuck out my hand. "Good luck, then."

He frowned. "And here I thought you were a sweet young thing. This is something Marjorie D'Lacorte might cook up."

"I will take that as a compliment." I stood. "Shall we keep walking? I see Maude and Orson up there."

He snatched my hand and shook it. Firmly. "All right. All right. It's a deal."

"You won't regret it!" I could have done a little jig right there on the boardwalk.

"Oh, I will," he said glumly. "I already do."

❦ 11 ❦

Tetrazzini Chickens Out

Hubbard Lands in City to Promote Boeing Airplane Company

By NED KIRK

SAN FRANCISCO, AUGUST 21: Eddie Hubbard, William Boeing's right-hand man, plans a short trip to this city to show off the Boeing C-700. "The seaplane is the future of aviation," the daring pilot proclaims. He will be in town this week to spread his aviation gospel and to take the braver of our city's bigwigs for aerial joyrides.

"Hattie! Hattie!" Raymond flagged me down. "Don't worry. He's gone."

Raymond seemed even fuzzier this morning than usual. Maybe he nipped at two bottles last night rather than one.

"Ned?" I asked. I couldn't think of any other "he." But he'd picked up everything I'd pulled together for him the morning before, when I got off work.

"Scruffy-looking guy. Needs a haircut. Grease under his nails." Raymond gave a tight nod, as if that was all that needed to be said about the unexpected visitor. "Asking for you. But I sent him on his way."

"Well, I do appreciate your watching out for me." I shifted the newspaper I carried to my other arm and pushed the button for the elevator. I was eager to catch a few precious winks, as Ned and I had a story to cover that afternoon.

Raymond stepped behind the front desk. "He wouldn't leave till I took this message." He handed me a piece of paper and I read the five words written there: "Mr. Whiskers' friend was here."

"Oh!" I stopped. "Do you know where he went?"

He scratched his head. "He did ask where to get a decent breakfast. I sent him over to Scuzzi's."

I flew upstairs to freshen up, then changed into the dress Ruby had bought for me. I popped on the matching cloche and hurried over to Scuzzi's.

The restaurant was crowded with workingmen, a crush of male heads all wearing similar newsboy-style caps. It took me a second or two to pick out the head I was looking for. Hoping for.

"Is that chair taken?" I stopped at the table for two where

Charlie sat by himself. Seeing him was like taking a long sip of cold water on a hot, hot day.

He stood and pulled the chair out for me. "I wasn't sure that fellow would give you my message. He didn't seem to think much of me."

"Raymond wasn't impressed with your dirty nails." I sat down. The waiter saw me, held up the coffee carafe, and waggled it, as if to ask if I wanted a cup. I nodded. I didn't really need any, but it would give me something to do with my hands.

"If he did anything but flit around behind that desk, he'd get his nails dirty, too." Charlie glanced down. "Guess they are kind of stained. But it comes with the territory."

I settled my dress. "That looks good." Charlie's breakfast of hash browns, eggs, bacon, and pie reminded my stomach that I'd skipped my wee-hours lunch to type another copy of my working-girls article.

When the waiter came with my coffee, Charlie ordered a second breakfast. "Eggs over medium this time," he told the waiter. "That's the way you like them, right?"

"Oh, I don't need all that," I protested.

"Yes, you do." He pushed the sugar bowl my way. "Perilee keeps fussing, worried that you're not eating. 'She'll be green-bean skinny,' she says." He looked me over. "You eat that breakfast or I'll tell her she's right."

I *had* been scrimping on meals so the coins in my cold cream jar would multiply faster. There had been a lot of saltine and butter sandwiches lately. Time to change the subject. "I read that Eddie Hubbard was coming to town." I thought it best not to mention that I knew the writer of the article. Or that I knew why he was in town.

"It's something a bright young reporter like you might be interested in." His eyes twinkled in that wonderful Charlie way.

The waiter placed my breakfast in front of me. My stomach clenched at the sight of it. I'd told Charlie about my job at the paper but had never gotten around to telling him what that job was. He had assumed I was a reporter. It was time to fess up.

"Charlie . . ."

"Don't you want your eggs?"

I took a bite. "Delicious." I might as well have sampled the tablecloth.

"I can't wait any longer." Charlie's face lit up like a starry night sky. "You've heard of Luisa Tetrazzini, the opera star, right?"

"Yes."

"Well, she's in town. Singing at some fancy theater." He gobbled down a biscuit in two bites. "And she's paid for an aerial tour of the city. Wouldn't have any pilot but Eddie Hubbard."

I poked at my fried eggs. "Your boss."

"And *he* wouldn't have any mechanic but me, so here I am." He pushed his empty plate out of the way and slid the piece of pie in its place. "Seemed like a great story in it for you."

Oh, this was awful. Here he was thinking about how he might be able to help me, and I hadn't even been honest with him. I cleared my throat to make sure I could trust my voice. "If the Great Tetrazzini's going up in the air, some news-hound has probably already sniffed it out."

"Maybe." Charlie cocked his head. "But maybe you'll sniff out something another newshound doesn't." He reached over and forked off a piece of my uneaten peach pie. How could I have forgotten about that scar over his left eye that dimpled when he smiled? "Cancel that. There's no 'maybe' when Hat-tie Brooks is on the case. Or whatever you call working a story."

I didn't deserve his faith in me. I set my fork down. "Char-lie. I have to tell you something." Everything spilled out.

"You stayed here to be a charwoman?" he asked when I'd finished. "You could have done that in Great Falls."

"I'm doing more than that," I said. "The research. And I do have the one baseball article. That's something I wouldn't have had in Great Falls."

He shook his head. "I gotta hand it to you. You really are going after this, aren't you?"

My heart melted at his kindness. His support. "I'm trying to," I told him.

"You done with your food?" When I nodded, he opened his wallet and threw down a dollar bill to pay for our break-fasts. "I suppose you'd already planned to be at the airfield."

"Yes." I stood up. "I'll see you there."

At the door, he took my hand. When his palm slid next to mine, it was like a key slipping into my heart. I squeezed. *One-two-three.* Like I used to do with Mattie. Charlie didn't know what that signal meant. Just as well.

"I have to say one thing, Hattie." He squeezed back, then looked right at me with those mesmerizing eyes. "I wish you'd been straight with me about the job. I think I deserved that."

I couldn't disagree with him. "I'm sorry. Truly sorry."

He tugged me close, and I filled my lungs with his clean smell. "If a guy wants to be your fellow, he'd best learn to watch out for those snake balls you keep throwing." His lips brushed my forehead. "I'll see you later."

After we parted company, I walked back to the hotel, his words of forgiveness buoying me up as if I were a zeppelin. If it hadn't been for my sturdy brown oxfords, I might have floated right away. How could I have forgotten how good Charlie smelled? How strong his hard-working hands? Or how being with him was like dipping into a beloved book? Maybe I had made a mistake. Maybe I should go to Seattle.

I stumbled over a stone on the sidewalk, jarring myself and my thoughts back to earth. My heart had no right to take over like this. It was a hammer making crooked nails out of all my plans to be a writer. Not a wife. I shot a cranky prayer heavenward, demanding to know why the good Lord had given Charlie Hawley eyes that made a girl forget everything she was working toward.

Back in my room, I pulled the covers over my head, aiming to get a few hours of shut-eye before the afternoon's event. There was little shut-eye but much tossing and turning. Finally I gave up and got dressed to go out again. Ned and I had planned to meet in the newsroom. But he was nowhere to be seen when I arrived. The minutes ticked past and still no Ned.

"Aren't you going to the airfield?" Miss D'Lacorte shrugged into a chiffon cocoon jacket.

I looked around. Was she speaking to me? Stunned at this attention from the Tiger Woman, I stammered out a reply. "I—I was supposed to go with Ned."

She opened her pocketbook, pulled out a set of car keys, and jingled them. "I'd say, don't look a gift horse in the mouth. Ride with me." She started for the elevator.

I hesitated. If I didn't leave soon, I'd miss the flight. But what would Ned think when he arrived to find me gone? If he arrived. Besides, did one dare turn down an invitation from a tiger?

"Wait!" I hurried after her, one step behind the whole way to her car.

"Got your notebook?" she asked as she cranked the ignition.

I was glad I could answer affirmatively. "I keep it in my pocketbook," I told her. A car honked as she lurched out into the street. I kept my eyes straight ahead. I hated to admit it, but Miss D'Lacorte made a good case against women having licenses to drive.

She took the next corner too sharply and sent a pedestrian scurrying back to the curb and me sliding up against the passenger door.

I pushed myself back to an upright seated position. "Are we late?" I hoped she'd hear the hint to slow down in my words.

"A reporter can never be too early." She shifted gears and we rolled down O'Farrell. "Or too well prepared." She glanced over at me. "I suppose it's hopeless to think you could write anything about Tetrazzini." The Tiger's claws unsheathed.

Thank goodness I'd thought to jot down some notes about the opera star when I'd been poking around in the morgue that time. I fished out my notebook and improvised. "Luisa Tetrazzini, called the Florentine Nightingale, was born June 29, 1871, and began singing opera as a child. She made her San Francisco debut in 1905. . . ."

Miss D'Lacorte held up one hand and gestured with the other. "Dry as—"

"Look out!" I flattened against the seat, steeling against a crash. She clasped the wheel and miraculously avoided hitting a jitney head-on.

"—dust," she continued, unfazed by the mayhem she was causing. "You need to add some frosting to those facts. Help them go down sweeter."

"She's large." I remembered her photograph in the paper. "Very large."

"Hattie." Miss D'Lacorte clicked her tongue. "And here I thought you actually had an imagination. What you mean to say is, 'The Florentine Nightingale is full-figured, attesting to a life lived with verve and passion.'"

I continued. "The neighbor's dog began to howl when I played one of her recordings on Maude's Grafonola." When it came to opera music, I sided with the dog.

"Her voice inspires each who hears to join the heavenly song," Miss D'Lacorte paraphrased. A long, heavy sigh escaped her. "You're not even trying."

I sat, chewing the end of my pencil as we rattled pell-mell

to the Flying Field at the Presidio. It was hard to think clearly when facing certain death due to either an auto wreck or the sharp tongue of Marjorie D'Lacorte. I thought about how dramatics defined Miss D'Lacorte's driving as well as her writing style. "How about this for the headline? 'Florentine Nightingale Soars Over San Francisco.'"

That earned me a quick glance. "Not bad. Now, give me the lead."

The lead? For a story yet to unfold? "I haven't met her yet. Haven't seen the flight!"

"Swizzle sticks. Never hurts to have a lead ready to go. Just in case." She double-clutched. "Sometimes we record history, but sometimes we make it."

I couldn't help but laugh. Me? Make history?

"I'm dead serious." She waggled her finger at me. "And you should be, too. I want one hundred words by the time we reach the airfield."

"A hundred!" I nearly dropped the pencil.

"This job's about quality *and* speed." She honked at the driver in front of her. "Now get cracking."

Okay. Okay. So what did I know? A fat—rather, a full-figured opera diva was going to go for a spin with Eddie Hubbard in one of Mr. Boeing's seaplanes. It would hardly do to comment about whether the plane would get off the ground with such a passenger. Opera singer. Airplane. Opera singer. Airplane. Opera singer . . . famous pilot! I began to scribble. With that germ of an idea, I was able to knit together words, then sentences, faster than Perilee could knit a pair of baby booties.

"We're nearly there." Miss D'Lacorte extended her arm to signal the last turn. "Whatcha got?"

"It's not very good," I started.

"I'll be the judge of that," she said. "Give."

"Here goes." I cleared my throat and then, hesitantly, began to read. "Each night on the stage, the Florentine Nightingale, Luisa Tetrazzini, sends her listeners soaring with her cultivated tones. Each day, from far-flung airfields, Eddie Hubbard sends airplanes soaring with his piloting skills. Today, history was made when opera singer and pilot soared together over our fair city, allowing Madame Tetrazzini to hit the highest note of her grand career."

The last word barely out of my mouth, I glanced over at Miss D'Lacorte. There wasn't any reaction right away. Then, one corner of her lipsticked mouth curved up. Ever so slightly. "You might not be worthless after all." With that pronouncement, she hurled the car into a parking spot near the airfield alongside a brand-new Packard. She turned off the engine, then shoved her door open, smacking it into the Packard. She looked at me and rolled her eyes. "Now the mayor will have one more thing to complain to Monson about!" She pulled out her handbag and shut the door. "Come on. That rat from the *Call* is already here."

I followed her, feeling very much like a lamb trotting after a shepherd. I was tempted to grab the hem of her cocoon coat so as not to get separated. A knot of people, mostly reporters armed with notepads and photographers with flashes at the ready, stood near an airplane. I jotted down the model number, pleased with myself that I'd remembered Charlie's aeronautics lessons. Painted yellow, the plane looked like an oversized kite awaiting a good gust of wind. It sported a pair of red pontoons, like giant-sized clown shoes. Three wavy stripes of red, white, and blue adorned the tip of the tailpiece.

A photographer stood on one of the pontoons for close-up shots. He was of average height and yet he was tall enough to look over the top of the plane's body. Could this flimsy machine really hold two people? Especially if one of them was the generously sized Luisa Tetrazzini?

There weren't many familiar faces in the crowd. At least, not familiar to me. Miss D'Lacorte seemed to know everyone. That must be Mr. Boeing, shaking hands with the mayor. Near them, Flash and another photographer jockeyed around one another for the best shots of the scene. The man off to the side, smoking and talking to Charlie as he worked on the plane, must be Eddie Hubbard. I weaved around a clump of reporters for a better view of Charlie at work.

There was no chance of my disturbing his endeavors. If he was occupied with a job that tickled his fancy, like working on planes, a body could dress like Helen of Troy and ride a mare backward, all the while singing "The Star-Spangled Banner," and Charlie would pay no never-mind. Of course, I had no room to talk. How many times had I headed to the morgue, intent on finding out something about Uncle Chester, unaware I'd worked through my midnight meal until my stomach put up a terrible ruckus? I had no idea what Charlie was doing with those tools over there, but he was doing it with fierce intensity.

My attention was diverted by a caravan of touring cars gliding toward the airfield. As soon as the first car came to a stop, a man wearing a top hat and evening jacket hopped out and scurried to the second. He opened the door and offered his hand. From that second car a very large woman emerged. She seemed to get stuck in the opening, but the man in the fancy dress gave a firm tug and she popped out, like a fat pickle from a small jar. *"Buon giorno!"* She waved a riding crop to the crowd. "Hello!"

This Florentine Nightingale had no trouble making herself heard. Two photographers ran at her, flash powder flaring in their Victor pans. "Oh, fine. That's Three-Alarm Dooley," Miss D'Lacorte said over her shoulder. "Let's hope he doesn't set the Great Tetrazzini on fire." She followed the rest of the reporters, far at the back, but soon she had grapevined her way through the crush, and there she was, right out front, right next to Luisa Tetrazzini.

The opera star was waving and smiling, but others in her retinue were not. In fact, soon there were emphatic gestures and shouts of "No, no!" I wiggled myself through the crush to Miss D'Lacorte's side. A little man wearing a beret was flapping his arms so fast and hard, I thought he might take off without benefit of an airplane.

"Madame's throat!" he cried. His words were echoed by Madame's contingent. "The wind, too cold! Too cold! And she must sing tomorrow night!"

"But it's August," someone pointed out. "And balmy."

"Down here, the balm." Mr. Beret pointed heavenward. "Up in the sky, who can tell?" He shivered for effect.

133

"So the air excursion is off?" Miss D'Lacorte pushed closer. "Too risky for the great Tetrazzini?"

Mr. Beret gestured again. "I am her manager. And I say this air no good for her voice. No good."

"No good. No flight?" repeated Miss D'Lacorte.

"*Si*. No flight!" Mr. Beret puffed himself up.

"But, *amore mio*," intoned the star, "I have already paid fifty dollars. So much money!"

Mr. Beret whisked his palms against each other, as if sweeping away that problem. Her foolish spending was clearly none of his affair. During this discussion, Charlie had been leaning against the side of the plane; he tugged on the bill of his cap when he saw me, then got back to his tinkering.

"Seems a shame to waste a flight." Miss D'Lacorte slapped her notepad shut, then called out to Eddie Hubbard. "You game regardless, Eddie?"

He did a double-take when he saw Miss D'Lacorte, then shrugged. "My time's bought and paid for." He flipped his cigarette butt to the ground and twisted it dead with his flight boot.

"Seems a shame to waste all this press, too," she continued.

Eddie Hubbard zipped up his flight jacket. "Do you have a point, Marjorie?"

Somehow it seemed fitting that this pilot would know her name. Part of her "interesting life," no doubt.

Miss D'Lacorte cocked her head. "How about a different passenger?"

"You?" Eddie Hubbard frowned. "That last time I took you up in Seattle, you—" He made an upchucking motion.

She held up her hand. "Not me. Her."

As if one body, the press corps swiveled their heads. In my direction.

My head swiveled, too. Was Miss D'Lacorte serious? She gave me a nod of encouragement. "Page one," she murmured, speaking the two words as if they were a magical incantation.

Charlie took his attention off readying the airplane for flight to see which sucker had been singled out as Tetrazzini's replacement. He grinned when he saw it was me.

I stood there for several seconds, my fear of the effects of gravity on that small craft battling the siren call of my own byline.

"Are we on?" asked Eddie.

I nodded, then turned to Miss D'Lacorte. "I guess I better come up with a new lead," I said. The crowd hooted as the Madame unzipped her flying costume and handed it over to me. The leather duster wrapped around me twice, and Charlie had to knot the goggles' strap to get them to stay on my head. I pulled gloves from the duster pocket and slipped them on my hands.

"Look here, Hattie!" I turned in the direction of Flash's voice. "That'll be a good one." I smiled for several of the other photographers, too.

"In bocca al lupo!" cried Luisa Tetrazzini.

"Um, thank you?" I said.

Her manager leaned toward me. "Very important. For good luck! You must say *crepi*!"

My pronunciation was nothing like his, but it did the trick and earned a huge smile from the manager and a roar of laughter from the opera star.

Eddie Hubbard helped me into the plane and I settled into the open compartment in front of the pilot's. I tried to convince myself it wasn't much different from riding in one of those Ferris wheel chairs, with nothing but a bar to hold you in. People didn't fall out of those, did they? If they did, I didn't want to know.

Charlie leaned into my compartment, tugging on this strap and that, making sure I was fastened in tight.

"Did you get whatever it was you were working on fixed?" I asked weakly.

"Mostly." He stepped back.

"Charlie!"

He grinned. "This is as safe as an auto," he said, patting the edge of my compartment. "I wouldn't let you go if it wasn't." He reached over and squeezed my gloved hand. The feeling that shot through me did nothing to help the jitters. My heart and my stomach leapfrogged over each other into my throat.

A deep inhale helped steady my nerves. I'd survived Miss D'Lacorte's wild motoring; surely I could survive one short jaunt through the sky. My heart's crazy flight was another story altogether, and one I'd have to deal with later.

"High-flying Hattie!" Flash cheered me on.

Miss D'Lacorte waved her notepad. "Happy landings!" she called.

Eddie climbed into the pilot's seat behind me and said

something I couldn't understand. Did he say to wave my arms? No time to wonder about it. Within a wink the engine grumbled to life, jogging me around in my seat despite being snugly strapped in.

Charlie slapped the side of the plane and gave Eddie a thumbs-up. Then he shifted slightly in my direction and snapped off a salute. I returned it with a quavery attempt of my own.

We backed away from the shore, made a long, clean turn to get going in the right direction, and then skimmed across the water's surface. So far, so good.

With forced bravado, I waved once more to the crowd, which I could no longer hear over the engine noise.

I squared myself in the seat. The seaplane looked even smaller from this inside view. The passenger compartment was about the size of the washtub I'd used for bathing back on the homestead. From where I sat, I could see things a mere mortal should never see: a rusted bolt, a mended tear in the body fabric, a seam that appeared to be unraveling.

"Oh, Lord," I prayed. "Keep me safe." I kept praying, vigorously, that my first-ever flight would not be my last.

The rumbling engine vibrated every part of my body, making me wonder if I'd return to earth with all my teeth. It was all I could do to keep a clumsy grip on my pencil and notepad. Slowly, awkwardly, like one of the gawky brown pelicans I'd seen on the bay, the man-made bird began to rise. I forced my eyes to open and my jaws to unclench as we gained speed and then altitude. One second we were skating on water, the next, on air.

We eased northward, toward the Yacht Harbor, clearing the main mast of a wooden schooner rocking in the marina there and startling a seagull resting on the rigging. As he flew off, complaining loudly about the disruption we'd caused, my stomach finally regained its proper place amongst my innards.

Lacy clouds frothed around the seaplane like spun sugar. We continued to push through to the clear sky above, and I pushed myself up in the seat, worries dissolving like the clouds. There was no room for fear when faced with such a vista. From my ever-ascending perch, I could take the city in all at once: the Palace of Fine Arts, the wharves, Nob Hill. And, if I crooked my neck, I could see the Golden Gate where the bay opened out to the Pacific Ocean. I'd have a crick later ' from all this gawking, but it'd be worth it.

The smoothness of this glide through the sky astonished me. After our bouncy beginning, I'd expected nonstop jostling. But now our progress was gentle enough for me to slip off my gloves and open my notepad to capture my thoughts. We nosed toward the Ferry Building, back to the place I'd first set foot in San Francisco. The sun formed diamonds on the bay's surface beyond the buildings and the busy wharves. With the wind rushing in my ears and scrubbing my face, I wrote down those words—"the sun formed diamonds"—and then crossed them right out. I could hear Miss D'Lacorte's sharp disapproval of that old cliché. I tried again. "The water glittered like a mother's loving eyes as she beholds her child. . . ." Another scratch-out. "Thousands of watery fireflies winked up at me from the surface of the bay. . . ." Watery fireflies? This was getting worse, not better. I put my pencil to paper once more. "It looked as if the bay were filled with crystal sequins, facets glimmering—"

My pencil gouged the page and I screamed. We were dropping! Falling. Out of the sky. I flapped my arms as if that activity would somehow slow our descent. Down, down, down. The water I'd admired seconds before was rising up to meet this bucket of bolts. Had the engine stalled?

"Eddie!" I screamed again, but the word was ripped out of my mouth by the rushing wind. Now we began to tip. To tilt. And still falling. I braced myself against the front of the compartment. Why had I so quickly volunteered for this? Pride! Pride that I would snag a story. Here was the fall that pride required. Loved ones' faces flashed in front of me. Even Aunt Ivy's.

San Francisco turned first on its side. Then upside down. Too frightened to be sick, I hung on for dear life. Mouth opened. No sound came out. We hurtled toward the Ferry Building. I called out again but this time for Charlie. The tower loomed in front of us. Dear God, don't let me die. Not now! I thought of Perilee. Of Charlie. Charlie and his thumbs-up. That image burned itself into the back of my eyes as if lit by flash powder. I prayed without words. Steeled myself for the crash. For the end. I closed my eyes.

A peculiar sensation overtook me. It was as if I were an infant again, being rocked in my mother's arms. My heart slowed its pounding. I opened my eyes.

San Francisco was proper side up. The sky above, the

sea below. We had nipped around the clock tower with room to spare. Once again we were cruising along, bobbing as gently as a bar of soap in a bathtub. I brushed at the tears that had leaked out under my goggles, then felt around for my notebook. Gone. Along with the borrowed gloves. I gulped sea air and laughed out loud at the antics of yet another agitated gull annoyed by our aircraft. I could see the crowd on the shore and hollered with sheer joy at the sight of them.

The pontoons kissed the water and we skimmed the bay's surface, coming to an easy rest back where we'd started. Eddie was quickly at my side, assisting me out of the seat.

"You are one cool customer," he said. "When I told you to wave your arms if you wanted some tricks, I didn't know you'd want the whole packet!"

Dazed, I tried to read his ear-to-ear grin. "The whole packet?"

He reached over and flipped up the collar on my loaned duster. "Loop the loop, spiral roll. We even did a falling leaf." He motioned for me to push my goggles up on top of my head. "You want to look jaunty for the camera," he said.

Jaunty. Tell that to my legs. Tell it to my stomach! But I squared my shoulders, wiped sweaty hands on my borrowed duster, and climbed out of the seaplane. We stood together on those clown-shoe red pontoons and I shook my clasped hands over my head like a victorious prizefighter.

I caught familiar newsroom faces in the crowd—Miss D'Lacorte, Flash. And Ned, too. When had he arrived? But Charlie was the first to greet me. I jumped on his neck and gave him a big kiss on the cheek. I didn't give a fig who saw. I was that glad to be alive. He swung me around. It was so wonderful, I didn't want to let go.

"Got a good story to tell, kid?" Miss D'Lacorte asked.

Charlie and I untangled and I smiled over at Eddie.

"You'll have to read about it in the papers," I answered.

❧ 12 ❧

Dora Dean Dives In

Too Cold for Tetrazzini to Fly
Dora Dean Takes Diva's Place

By DORA DEAN

SAN FRANCISCO, AUGUST 22: It may cost me three dollars to hear Tetrazzini sing, but it cost her fifty dollars to see me fly.

Mr. Monson was thrilled with my flying escapade write-up. "Page two!" Gill exclaimed.

"But it says, 'By Dora Dean,'" I pointed out. "No one will know it's me." Surviving the flight with Eddie had emboldened me to ask Mr. Monson to file the story under my own name. His response was to switch his cigar to the other side of his mouth.

"Still, you've made the big time." Gill rolled up his shirt-sleeves. "Got a deadline!" He began clacking away on his typewriter. From across the newsroom, Miss D'Lacorte toasted me with her coffee cup.

Congratulations had been showered on me from all quarters: the elevator operator, Spot and Bernice, even Percy, the night watchman. A large dose of quiet emanated from one particular desk, however. Ned had offered a brief explanation for his tardiness—a flat tire—but not one word of congratulations. I didn't want anything to fester between us, so I took the bull by the horns the day after the article appeared. I poured two cups of coffee and marched over to his desk.

"Buy you a cup of java?" I asked, extending one of the cups.

At first, he pretended to be too intent on his typing to notice me. So I lifted the cup over the typewriter and slowly, slowly tipped it, as if to spill it out on his machine.

"What are you doing?" He grabbed it away.

"Trying to get your attention." I smiled.

"*I'm* working," he said.

"Don't you have five minutes?" I frowned. "For a friend?"

"You're right." He reached out and clinked cups with me. "I suppose you want congratulations."

"Well, that'd be nice, of course, but what's more important to me is that we're square." I leaned against his desk. "Why am I getting the silent treatment?"

"I've been busy." He cut his eyes down to the typewriter keys.

"So that's all?"

He shrugged. "All I want to talk about for now."

"I didn't know where you were . . . ," I started.

143

"I'm glad you got to the airfield," he said. "I'm not mad that you didn't wait for me."

"Then what are you mad about?"

He typed a few more words. I waited.

"Who was the flyboy?" He stopped and looked at me.

"Flyboy?" I thought for a second. "Oh, you mean Charlie. He's a friend from high school, in Iowa."

"Friend?" Ned raised an eyebrow.

"Yes." My answer came out sharper than I intended. Charlie was certainly a friend. And whatever else there was to it was none of Ned's beeswax. Especially since I barely knew myself.

"Okay then." He nodded. "Okay." Then he grinned. "That's great. Now I really do have to get back to work."

I gathered my things and headed to the Cortez for a short nap before my supper date with Charlie.

Raymond had two messages for me when I arrived at the hotel. The first was one Ruby had sent over. Pearl had taken another turn—"By the time you read this, I'll be on my way to Santa Clara," she'd written. This time, Pearl needed a specialist. "I know I haven't paid you back yet for the other loan, but if there is any way you can help, financially, I would be so grateful." I thought of my Pond's Cold Cream jar and how it had acquired a nice little jingle. At this rate, what with helping Ruby out, I might never make a trip to Seattle. I was instantly ashamed of my selfishness. The important thing was Pearl's health. I went upstairs to change into my yellow dress and then gathered what I needed to wire Ruby the money. I would do it after supper.

The second message was from Mrs. Holm wondering if I had Ruby's mother's telephone number. She had a question for Ruby about a recent transaction. I rang right back and told her I only had a mailing address. Long-distance calls were out of my budget. "Oh, of course," Mrs. Holm said. "I'm so sorry to have bothered you."

Charlie met me in the lobby, armed with copies of the paper he'd collected from all the pilots at the airfield. "For your scrapbook," he said.

"For Dora Dean's scrapbook," I corrected. But I was still pleased at the thought. And pleased to have someone like Charlie to share my good news.

He set his cap on the front desk in the lobby. "Mr. Hubbard gets all the credit for his fancy flights, but I know I'm part of the reason he's up in the air," he said. " 'Not for glory, but for the job well done,' " he added dramatically, quoting our old teacher, Miss Simpson.

I whacked him with one of the newspapers.

"Ow!" He rubbed his head. "Maybe I should reconsider that offer of supper."

"It'd take more than a clop with the *Chronicle* to harm that hard head of yours." I shuffled the papers he'd given me into a manageable bundle. "Let me run these upstairs. I'm famished."

Charlie plopped his cap back on his head. "I'll wait right here."

I hurried up to my room and dropped off the papers. A quick glance in the mirror afforded a pleasant surprise: the girl there looked like she was on her way somewhere.

Somewhere besides a cleaning woman's job. She looked like she had another good story or two in her. I smiled at the thought. A story or two and maybe even a real job at the paper. I let myself enjoy that notion for a minute, then locked up and rode the elevator down to meet Charlie.

Supper flew by in a barrage of Charlie stories. As tired as I was, I kept him talking. I was like a squirrel, storing up his voice for the coming winter. When the last of our sandwiches were devoured—minced olive for me, a club for him—I stifled a yawn.

"I guess I'm boring you," he teased.

"Never." Another yawned threatened. "But I didn't get a nap in today." I made a motion as if dusting a shelf. "One of the many necessities of working the night shift if I change my schedule."

"Oh, I'm sorry." He stood, then came around to pull out my chair. "I didn't even think about that."

"I'll live," I assured him. "I'll catch up on my beauty sleep tomorrow."

He offered me his arm and I took it, and we stepped out onto the sidewalk. "Let's head this way," I said. "I have an errand."

Charlie stopped and made a fearful face. "Not at a hat shop?" he asked. "Or some such?"

"Rest easy." I rolled my eyes at him. "I wouldn't make you suffer through something like that." Nor would *I* want to suffer through shopping of any kind with Charlie moping behind me.

"I'm going to mail a copy of your article back home, to Mother and Dad," Charlie said. "They'll be so proud of you."

"Well, don't make too big a fuss," I said. "It might be a fluke."

He guided me around a grandmother pushing a pram. "I think that Miss Marjorie D'Lacorte needs to take care that Miss Hattie Brooks doesn't pass her right on by."

I shook my head. "She has no reason to fret." I shivered a bit. The evening breeze carried a touch of fall's cool air in it. My jacket might get me through autumn, but after that, I'd need something warmer. And the cheapest winter coat at Praeger's would be well out of my price range after I wired Ruby the money for Pearl's specialist. I crossed my fingers for some more research assignments. "Even if I got a job at the paper, it'd be on the fashion desk or society news. I wouldn't be a *real* reporter."

"Wasn't it Lincoln who said 'Whatever you are, be a good one'?" Charlie patted my hand. "You'd hit a home run no matter which job you were given."

"Spoken like a true friend," I said lightly. A hank of his dark hair had fallen over his forehead. I brushed it back. "You need a haircut," I teased.

He caught my hand. "What I really need is to know if what you want is here in San Francisco."

I pulled away. It seemed Charlie and I had just figured out how to be easy with one another again, and now this. "Let's not talk about this now. Here."

"I want to." He stopped under the Owl Drug awning. "I'm tired of not talking about it."

Something in his voice made me stop, too. "I'm not ready—"

"I know. I know." He exhaled deeply. "That I can live

147

with. But what I can't live with is wondering if you'll ever be ready. For me, that is."

It was a fair question. What was the answer?

He didn't wait for me to say anything. "You know I'd be the last person to keep you from doing what you want."

"I do know that."

He reached out and took my hands in his. "What about the papers in Seattle?" he asked. "Couldn't you try to get a job at one of those?"

Another fair question. "Yes. And no." I stepped closer to him. Bad mistake. His eyes had too much power at this range. Not letting go of his warm, strong hands, I rocked back on my heels, away from those eyes. "I could try, certainly. But it'd be like planting a whole new field, from scratch." I paused, thinking about what to say next. "Here, it's like I've already picked the rocks and done the plowing. Now all I have to do is buy the seed."

He edged closer. A matronly woman clucked her tongue at us. "Really," she said, the word dripping with disapproval. We walked a few more feet, then turned down a street with fewer passersby.

"What about Chase and the little girls? Fern and Lottie?" he asked. "They all miss you like crazy."

I slowed my pace for a moment. "I miss them, too." That was the truth. Little Lottie wouldn't even know me by the time I got to see her. "It's not that I don't love them or want to be with them. . . ."

He stopped to face me, placing his hands on my coat sleeves. "It's me that you don't want to be with." His voice was soft. Sad. Maybe even resigned.

"Everything's all jumbled in my head." I blinked back tears. "It's like I've got all these quilt pieces—Perilee and the kids, Seattle, the newspaper. And I can hardly leave Ruby now, not with Pearl so sick and all."

"Am I even *one* of the quilt pieces?"

I swiped at my eyes. A life without Charlie? It was impossible to imagine. "Yes. You are certainly an important piece of my life."

"Well, that's a comfort," he said with a head shake. "Look, I saw that guy with Miss D'Lacorte. He's a reporter, too, right? Is that my competition?"

"Ned?" Ned was barely speaking to me. "No. No." How could I explain things to Charlie when I wasn't even sure myself? "Looking back, I'd have to agree with Aunt Ivy that I was a fool to think I could prove up on Uncle Chester's homestead. I'd never farmed and didn't have one idea about what that big prairie could be like."

"Don't be too hard on yourself," Charlie said. "Lots of men went bust out there, too."

"That's just it." His words helped jell my thoughts. "I *was* hard on myself. At first. For failing." We started walking again. "Did you know that Thomas Edison made thousands of mistakes before he got the lightbulb right?"

"Thomas Edison?" Charlie wrinkled his brow.

"Yes, and even that Ty Cobb strikes out, sometimes, too, doesn't he?"

He shook his head. "This sounds like one of those try, try, and try again lectures Miss Simpson used to give."

"Not exactly." Why was it I could hear the explanation so clearly in my mind but the words were coming out all

149

knotted up like tangled thread? "It's sort of about not giving up. But more, it's about giving yourself—giving *my*self the chance to see what I'm really made of." I thought back to the emptiness I'd first felt after leaving Vida. That feeling that something was unfinished. That *I* was unfinished. "It probably makes no sense to you, but I don't think I'll be able to know what I can really do with my life unless I stick it out."

He didn't say anything for about a half a block. "And your only shot is here?"

His question pricked like a darning needle. "It is for now."

We slowly crossed the street, as if each of us were carrying a steamer trunk on our backs. Or in our hearts. "Oh, here's Western Union." I unclasped my pocketbook and brought out my wallet.

"You need to wire money?" He reached out to open the office door for me.

"To Ruby. Pearl needs a specialist."

"But you told me you already gave her some money." He stood so that he blocked my entry. "Doesn't seem right, her asking again."

"Charlie!" I tapped him to make him step aside. "A little girl needs my help." I hadn't been able to help Mattie. There was no way I'd let Pearl down.

"Okay. Okay." He brushed that rebellious hank of hair off his forehead. "I better be getting back. We're leaving in the morning."

"Back to Seattle?" My heart felt as if it'd been put in an icebox. "So soon?"

He turned up his hands. "Seems like there's not much reason to stick around."

"Charlie—"

"You know I wish the best for you. But I may have to start thinking about what's best for me. I'm sure you can understand that."

I wanted to say, "But what does that mean, the best for you?" I wanted to say, "I'll look for a job in Seattle." I wanted to say, "Don't leave now." But all of that stayed locked up inside. Instead I said, "It was so very good to see you, Charlie. Thank you for the meals and for—for everything. Good-bye." I held out my hand to shake.

He clasped it, stepping close. I thought he was going to kiss me again, right there in front of Western Union! Would I be able to say good-bye if he did? Seconds passed.

There was no kiss. He released my hand, strode down the steps to the sidewalk, and, with that cap of his, was soon folded into the crowd of other workingmen in their matching caps and I could not see which way he went.

"Are you going inside?" a woman on the steps behind me asked.

"Oh, yes. Pardon me." I stepped into the lobby, my shoes making a lonely scuffing sound as I walked to the nearest operator window.

❧ 13 ❧

Shaken to the Core

September 4, 1919

Dear Ruby,

Oh, what a blessing that the new medicine seems to be helping Pearl. You must be so relieved. It will be good to see you whenever you return. And the thought that you might be able to bring Pearl with you makes this absence from you easier to bear.

The person you asked about is a frequent supper guest at Perilee's, she informs me. I do not hear from him myself. Until I do, I feel the only honorable thing is for me not to write him, either.

Ned has taken a keener interest in my work. He makes a carbon copy of one of his articles each day and tasks me to be his copy reader. This is a better writing

*education than anything Miss Simpson devised. Allow
me to crow a bit and tell you that he used one of my
phrasings just the other day—"Pinkerton detectives are
in the pink in phony ruby scheme." It gave me quite the
thrill to see that silly sentence in print. As much as I
enjoy Bernice and Spot, I do long for the day I trade in
my navy blue smock for a (working!) typewriter.*

*If there is anything I can do for you here, please let
me know.*

*Yours,
Hattie*

The latest from Ruby sounded like she would be back in town
in a few weeks and Pearl would arrive in October, which
would make a wonderful early birthday present for me. But
it also meant I needed to hurry up and finish Pearl's quilt. I
took it to work to stitch on during my lunch hour.

"What's that you're working on?" Spot asked. "It's so
cheery."

"It's for Ruby's daughter, Pearl." I spread the quilt top out
so Spot could see the whole thing. "But I've got to get busy.
Sounds like she'll be here soon."

"Grandmother's Fan," Bernice observed, looking at the
pattern. "Have you extra needles?"

And that was the beginning of our wee-hours quilting bee.
Spot was enthusiastic but a bit uneven. For someone so solid,
Bernice took the tiniest stitches. With a needle in hand, she
became another person and nearly talked circles around Spot
each night as we sewed.

Because of the quilting project, the only time spent in

the morgue was for other people's projects. Though Ned had helped as much as he could, I was still straddling two worlds—that of charwoman and reporter hopeful. I was weary of my late-night sweeping and scouring and ready to take on the mantle of cub reporter. But my aerial story had not been enough to convince Mr. Monson; I needed something even more dramatic or I would never be able to plant my feet firmly under a newsroom desk. I must be as bold as an eagle or be resigned to the life of a crow, hopping after the bits and crumbs left by others. One night, I decided to forgo a few hours' sleep and head straight to the morgue instead of home to my bed after work.

Fighting against scratchy eyelids, I pulled down yet another bound journal of back issues and began to read. The columns of newsprint blurred together. I found myself nodding off. This would not do! I pinched my cheeks to wake myself up and marched back and forth along the floor, swinging my arms vigorously to get the blood flowing. After several minutes of these gymnastics, I took my seat again and picked up where I left off.

Another hour passed. Another round of marching and arm-swinging. I was generally a hopeful person, but it seemed to me I had taken on a task that made setting fence posts in the frozen prairie seem simple. These pages and pages and pages of newsprint were filled with names and dates and events. Here was a report about Harry Houdini's famous escape from a straitjacket; there an article recounting the progress made so far on the new Lincoln Memorial, in Washington, D.C; the sinking of the *Lusitania;* Babe Ruth's first home run. Why did I think that in this enormous tangle of human doings, I would find out anything else about Uncle Chester, let alone anything newsworthy?

I slammed the big volume shut and lugged it over to the bookcase. As I began to slide it back in its proper spot, I noticed I'd accidentally folded in a corner of a section of pages. Balancing the heavy book on my left hand, I flipped it open to smooth out the bent sheets. My fingers passed over a headline in the right-hand column, near the bottom of the page: "Bank Is Victim of $4,550 Forgery." From under the headline, Uncle Chester's name leaped out. "Chester Hubert Wright is accused of attempting to cash a forged bank draft, drawn on the National Park Bank of New York and in the amount of $4,550. Wright claimed the check was given him by a friend."

My arms could no longer hold the book. I set it on the library table, reading the horrible article through several more times. When Uncle Chester had called himself a scoundrel in his only letter to me, I'd believed it a bit of poetic license. My throat tightened to think that the same person who had given me a chance at a life of my own was nothing more than a thief. And not a very good one, either, or he would not have gotten caught.

I returned the heavy leather volume to the shelf, then sat in the dark for a good long while, batting at my discovery as a cat might a ball of yarn. Like me, Uncle Chester had been orphaned at a young age, out on his own before most boys are out of short pants. It wasn't impossible to imagine him falling in with the wrong crowd and embracing a life outside

155

of respectable society. But that seemed something out of a Horatio Alger novel, too pat to be true. My uncle had filled his claim shack with books—was that the action of a thief? And he was held in such high regard back in Vida! Perilee, who had no tolerance for the slick and sinful, had nothing but good to say about him. How could he have fooled her? Or Leafie? Or Rooster Jim?

Speaking of fools, I had proved myself one, once again, with a silly idea that a story about my uncle might be my ticket to a press card. I hadn't thought it through, hadn't thought about the consequences should I learn, as I had, that Uncle Chester deserved that scoundrel label. My investigating had provided a powerful lesson: truth can both lift up and knock down. With one blow, the truth about my uncle had destroyed two dreams. I had no stomach for learning anything more about his life. I would close up Pandora's box as tightly as I could, even if that meant I might never find the story that would admit me to the rank of reporter. Why did I keep hitching myself to dreams as big as that Montana sky? I was like Rooster Jim's chickens, with no way to fly that high.

I trudged up to the lobby. Ned was coming in as I was going out; he called a greeting to me but I walked on as if I hadn't heard. I feared that if I opened my mouth, even to say hello to someone, Uncle Chester's story would come spilling out. I needed some time alone to mull over what to think, what to feel.

There had been someone I could confide in, someone who would understand. Charlie. But by staying here, I'd built a fence between us that might never find its gate. As I walked, the pain of that choice throbbed like a sore tooth. Every few steps, I'd poke at it to see if it still hurt. It did.

Uncle Chester had set me off balance inside, but something was off balance outside, too. It wasn't until I came upon a feather that I realized what was wrong, and scanned the sky. Generally, the gulls could make themselves heard over any traffic noises. But I heard no *maaw-maaw-maaws*. Odder yet, I didn't see any gulls above. Still, I picked up the feather for my growing collection. Maude had teased that soon I'd have enough for wings of my own.

Admiring a pyramid of oranges on display at the corner grocer, I missed my step and stumbled. I fought to keep my feet under me, realizing I hadn't stumbled—the sidewalk was bucking like a cranky range horse.

Juggling oranges as they bounced wildly around on his display, the shopkeeper shouted, "Earthquake!"

The drugstore sign above us swung wildly. A horse whinnied. Someone screamed. Was it me? I held tight to a lamppost while the earth went mad. Buildings groaned. Windows rattled. Cable cars came to a screeching halt. Finally, the shaking stopped, as abruptly as it had started.

I relaxed my grip on the post. "Is it over?" I looked at Mother's watch, pinned to my bodice: 1:16.

The shopkeeper scrambled to recover his escaped fruit. A street urchin helped himself to a pair of oranges and took off running. For some reason, I began to laugh so hard that tears flowed down my cheeks.

"You all right, miss?" The shopkeeper paused in his clean-up efforts to look me over. "First time?"

I wiped the tears from my cheeks, nodding.

"Well, that was a pretty good one." He looked around. "Don't see much damage. Looks like it's nothing to worry about."

Within minutes, the sidewalk and street were full of people comparing notes. The china shop lost three teapots. "Spode," said the manager with a sigh.

"I've lost my spectacles." A frail older woman wandered in my direction, her hat askew and a bump on her nose. "Something fell off the building there." She made a brushing gesture across her face. "Knocked them clean off."

"Are you hurt?" I asked.

"I don't think so." But her hands trembled as she attempted to right her hat. I helped her inside the drugstore whose sign still creaked and moaned overhead. The store was a clatter of loud voices and frenetic activity. I stepped over a broken bottle of Vinol cod liver oil and stooped to pick up a few boxes of Rexall Cold Tablets, spilled from the shelf. "May I have a glass of water for my friend?"

The man behind the soda fountain set a glass on the countertop while I helped the woman onto a stool.

"Here." I held the glass as she took a sip. "Drink it up."

"All quiet now," said the counterman. "Just a jolt to get the juices going. Doesn't look like anything too serious."

The lady smiled weakly. "I'd rather get my jolt from coffee." She rummaged in her pocketbook, found an embroidered handkerchief, and blew her nose. "Thank you, my dear. I'll be all right now."

"Are you sure? Without your spectacles?"

"Oh, it's a bit of a blur, but I can manage." She patted my hand. "Don't you worry."

I helped her off the stool, then went back out on the street. Everyone had a story to tell. And I was there to listen, notepad in hand. The young man in the paisley bow tie said he'd been thrown right off the cable car by the jolt. A little girl's best Mary Janes shook right off her feet. The banker in a pin-striped suit had been on the seventh floor of his building when the earthquake hit. He kept repeating, "It was as if I were swinging in a hammock, back and forth, back and forth." I collected twenty or thirty stories; then I did what any good reporter would do. I called them in.

When I finished reading off my notes to him, Mr. Monson said, "Well done, young lady. Well done."

The next morning, I found mention of the earthquake on page four. Someone, maybe the copy reader, had compiled notes from different reporters into one measly column inch of text:

> The heaviest earthquake in several years rocked the East Bay around one o'clock yesterday afternoon. Aside from a rattling of windows and dishes, no damage was reported, although occupants of area skyscrapers reported a sensation of swinging as in a hammock.

I would never get credit, but it felt good to know that I—and the pin-striped banker—had contributed in some small way to the news.

Still, I couldn't help but think that while the city of San Francisco had experienced one earthquake on September 4, 1919, I had experienced two. The earth's rumbling and reeling had done no real damage. But the other earthquake, the truth about Uncle Chester, had left marks that might never be repaired.

§ 14 §

War of Words

September 6, 1919

Dear Perilee,

You may have heard about the earthquake here—my first, and I wouldn't mind if it was my last. I still feel a bit shaky, but I suppose that's to be expected.

Don't feel you have to read the enclosed, but I made you a carbon copy of my women in the work world series. Last night, I finished typing up copies for each of the girls I interviewed; you, and they, will no doubt be the only readers. Regardless, I do feel proud of my efforts. Oh, I almost forgot to tell you—I caught the Tiger Woman's attention the other night. She was roaring at the new cub reporter about something he'd written. "You." She

pointed to me. "What does one include in every lead?" I
meekly answered, "Who, what, where, when, and why."
She turned to the poor reporter and snarled, "Don't they
teach anything in those colleges?" The reporter slunk out
of the room and wasn't seen for two days.

There is a farewell party tonight for the Varietals,
Maude included. She says this is her last road trip and
the diamond on her left ring finger is proof of that.
Orson seems like a fine fellow; I'm so very happy for both
of them.

Ruby is still in Santa Clara, but it looks like she'll
be back in another week or so. With Bernice and Spot's
help, Pearl's quilt is finished. I can't wait to give it
to her!

Your friend,
Hattie

P.S. Do you think I should send a copy of my series to
Charlie? I don't know, as my only Seattle mail comes
from you.

Rereading what I'd written, I felt a tiny twinge of guilt for
holding back what I'd learned about Uncle Chester. Though
I might feel less unburdened in the telling, what I knew
would only hurt Perilee, or whichever of his old friends I
might choose to confide in. Thank goodness Ruby was still
out of town! I would need time before I could face her without wearing such bad news on my face. Aunt Ivy used to say
if something's big enough to worry about, it's big enough

to pray about. So that was what I did as I crawled into bed. "Lord, you can't change my uncle's past," I prayed, "but could you please help me forgive him?"

A few short hours later, I rousted myself from bed. My work schedule had turned me into a night owl; I was rarely up before two or three in the afternoon. But I was eager to give each of the girls I'd interviewed a copy of *Female 49ers: San Francisco Women Who Find Gold in Their Work*. The copies never would have gotten typed if it hadn't been for Ned. One night when there had been no research assignments for me, he'd patiently demonstrated the Rational Typewriting Method. Once I mastered a feel for the home keys, it was a snap to get the rest of the Rational Method. Typing up copies of each *Female 49ers* article provided the perfect means for transforming me from hunt-and-pecker to confident master of the keyboard. It took only a few evenings—and one wastepaper basket full of failed efforts—to accomplish my objective. And now I was eager to gift each interview subject with a copy of her own story.

My first stop was the Fairmont. Florence, one of the hotel maids, had helped me search Miss Clare's room one time when a favorite kid leather glove had gone missing. It was Florence who'd thought to pull out the dresser drawers, and there it was, stuck inside the frame. When I found her and gave her the copy of the article, you would have thought I was giving her the key to the city. She read it right then and there. "You make me sound like somebody," she said, teary-eyed.

"Well, you are somebody," I told her.

She shook her head. "Not to most folks."

"You know this might never get published," I said.

"That's no nevermind." She pressed the paper to her chest. "Just seeing these words here makes me hold my head higher." I couldn't think of anything that had ever made me feel so proud.

I passed Praeger's on the way to my next delivery and paused for a little window-shopping. Admiring the latest gabardine outfits on display, I couldn't help but think of Ruby. The good thing about window-shopping is that it is easy on the pocketbook. I decided Ruby would look stunning in the emerald-green ensemble with the shawl collar and made a mental gift of it to her. And the dove-gray number might suit me. It would be the perfect thing to wear to Maude's going-away dinner. Perfect, except for the price tag. My faithful yellow dress and jacket would have to do. I turned away from the shop window with a sigh, not so much about not being able to afford a new gown, but suddenly feeling a bit out of sorts and alone, in spite of Florence's kind words. With Ruby gone and Maude busy wrapping things up in preparation for her road trip, I hadn't had much female companionship recently. Not that I didn't enjoy Bernice and Spot, but they were work colleagues. They'd helped me with Pearl's quilt, but I couldn't call them social friends. It'd been a long while since I'd enjoyed girl talk over a soda at the drugstore. Or seen the latest romantic comedy at a Sunday matinee. Or curled up with a cup of tea and a sewing project, both made sweeter because of the company.

The final stop on my itinerary was at the hospital where

Spot's sister, Tinny, worked. A sharply starched matron frowned when I asked where I might find her, but grudgingly directed me to the proper floor. I waited while Tinny finished ministering to a patient and then gave her the article. I'd saved her for last because I felt the piece I'd written about her was my very best. Perhaps it was a bit flowery, but I'd compared her to Joan of Arc. There was something so pure and purposeful about her. Ten minutes in her company, you wanted to give your own life over to helping others. Not that she was a saint, like Joan. Tinny's language could be a bit colorful, and I had it on reliable authority from Spot that Tinny used her knowledge of chemistry to manufacture gin in their basement laundry tub. These latter details did not appear in my piece, for obvious reasons. One of the best quotes from all the girls came from Tinny: "If we weren't meant to reach out to others, we'd not been given a pair of hands."

When she came out of the patient's room, her face lit up with a warm smile. "Well, if it isn't our own Nellie Bly," she said. "What are you doing here?"

I handed her the article and she read it there in the hospital hallway. She didn't say anything for a moment when she finished, just folded it up and put it in her pocket. Then she looked me straight in the eye. "The next thing you bring me will be a newspaper clipping," she said. "With your name front and center."

"What a dreamer you are," I said, shaking my head. Tinny had no idea about my painful discoveries—about Uncle Chester and about myself. At least she believed I could still be a reporter. "But it's not up to me."

She pointed her finger at me. "Of course it is! Who else is going to make it happen?"

"Well, I am doing my best."

Another nurse had come up to us and was obviously trying to get Tinny's attention. "You better get back to work," I said.

"I'll be right there," Tinny said to the other nurse. She took a step down the hall, then turned back to me, patting her pocket. "Your best doesn't belong in here. It belongs on the page. 'Fortune befriends the bold.'" She winked. "Emily Dickinson." With that, she was gone, and I was left to ponder her admonition as I made my way out of the hospital. I wasn't sure how I could work harder. Tinny simply didn't understand. My fate was in Mr. Monson's hands. Not my own.

A church bell somewhere chimed the hour. There was time enough for a hot bath before the evening's outing. I splurged on a cable-car ride back from the hospital and was soon at the hotel. Maybe I'd even use some of those lilac bath salts Maude had given me. With my mind on such weighty matters, I wasn't immediately aware of my name being called. "Miss Hattie!" From her tone, Sadie the day clerk had evidently been attempting to get my attention for some time.

"I'm sorry," I said. "My mind was somewhere else."

"You got a telephone call." She handed me a slip of paper with a number written on it. "A Mr. Monson. Says to ring him back. Right away."

"Mr. Monson?" My light spirits turned to lead. How had he gotten my number? Oh, who cared about that! Why was he calling? On a Saturday? It couldn't be good news. No. It was bad news. Had to be. My newsroom stint must be over. At least I still had the cleaning job.

"Shall I get the operator for you?" Sadie asked.

"Operator?" He had said to phone right away. "Oh. Yes."

Sadie peered over the desk at me. "Maybe you'd like to use the phone in the back office."

"I would. Thank you." That would be so much better than learning I was being fired out here in the open, in the lobby. "That's kind of you."

I followed her to the office and sat in the wooden chair by the telephone.

"Don't touch anything," she cautioned. "And make it quick."

I nodded, then shakily gave the operator Mr. Monson's number. After three rings on the other end, I heard his gruff "Hello?"

"Mr. Monson?" I squeaked out. "This is Hattie Brooks. You phoned?"

"Brooks." He mumbled the name as if he were trying to place me. "Brooks. Fine name for a byline," he said.

This was a funny way to get fired. What was I supposed to say? Thank you?

"So how did it come to you?" he asked. "A bit unorthodox."

I had no idea what he was talking about. And I wasn't clever enough to play along as if I did. Taking a deep breath, I confessed my confusion. "I'm sorry, sir, I don't think I understand."

Even over the telephone line, I could hear him chewing on

his ever-present cigar. I wondered if he ever lit them. "Female 49ers," he said impatiently. "Though why you gave it to Marjorie rather than me, I can't imagine."

I sat hard against the back of the chair. "Miss D'Lacorte had my article?" I'd given away all the copies I'd typed, except for the one in my desk in my room at the hotel.

"Neither here nor there. Can't say I was sold on the idea at first, but seems like the sort of thing to draw in female readers." He coughed. "New female readers. Here's what I'd like to do: run each of the eight pieces over eight Sundays. What do you say?"

He liked my article. He was going to publish it! Wait till I told Bernice and Spot. And Tinny! Tinny. Her words rushed back at me. *Fortune befriends the bold.* I swallowed. Hard. Maybe I had lassoed that dream. "I'd say that sounds like you're offering me a job. A reporter's job." I squinched my eyes and waited for the explosion from the other end of the line.

It didn't come. "I'd say you're right." He chuckled. "Though Lord help us with you and Marjorie in the same office. We men will be outnumbered."

A tear wriggled its way out of my left eye and dripped on the handset. "I accept," I said, trying not to sniffle into the telephone.

"Then plan on starting Monday. I'll let the employment office know that they have a spot to fill on the cleaning crew. And that we have a new cub reporter."

Reporter! For the *San Francisco Chronicle.* Wouldn't Perilee just pop! Ruby, too! This was news I would even share with Charlie, whether he wrote back or not. I had to let him know that it had been worth it after all. I thanked Mr. Monson, and we said good-bye. I replaced the receiver, but sat with my hand resting on it for several minutes, trying to take it all in. I'd written a story with a San Francisco hook. One good enough to catch an editor's attention. Would I dare ever ask Miss D'Lacorte how she'd gotten hold of it? Maybe. But not right away.

I practically floated to the restaurant for the farewell party. Maude looked stunning in her newly bobbed hair and flapper-style sheath. The pearls around her neck hung nearly to her knees. When I made my way over to her, Orson was tugging on the strand. "This makes a handy leash," he said. "Maybe I'll hang on so tight you won't be able to leave."

"But, darling, I must," she said. "That way you can miss me all the more." They both laughed, and Maude dragged Orson to the dance floor.

"There you are!" Ned was at my side. "Thought you'd never get here."

"I'm not even late," I said. "Don't be silly."

"Come on. We're over this way." At the table, he held out my chair for me and then sat to my right. "You are positively glowing tonight."

I was bursting to tell my news, but this was Maude's evening. The spotlight should be fully on her. Besides, it might be more fun to surprise Ned on Monday morning. And would he be surprised!

"A penny for your thoughts," he said.

"Oh, I'm just thinking about Monday." I smiled, pressing back a giggle.

"Monday? No, no, no." He pretended to knock on my

head. "Absolutely not. This is Saturday night, a time for fun and frivolity. Not work."

I smiled again. "I will force myself to have fun and be frivolous."

"That's the spirit." The waiter came by and Ned ordered two ginger ales. Maude and Orson joined us, Maude's cheeks flushed pink from dancing.

"What are you two sticks in the mud doing here?" she demanded. "Out on the dance floor."

"By orders of Her Majesty," Orson piped in. Maude stuck her tongue out at him.

"Oh, I'm a terrible dancer," I said. "Two left feet and all that."

Ned stood and extended his hand to me. "Then we will make the perfect partners." He lifted me to my feet and out on the dance floor for a waltz.

"Shame on you for being such a liar," I told him. "You're a wonderful dancer."

"Only because I have a wonderful partner." He drew me closer. My stomach did a little flip. But I didn't push away. In fact, I leaned my cheek on his lapel. The wool was warm and soft against my skin. "This is nice," I murmured.

He tilted my head up. "Very nice." The band finished the waltz number but we stayed on the dance floor. I thought we were doing the fox-trot but I really wasn't sure. I simply followed Ned's lead.

"I could get used to having you for a partner," Ned said.

"We do manage fairly well together," I said as we negotiated a turn.

"I was thinking beyond the dance floor. And the news-room."

I nodded. I knew what he'd been thinking. "Ned, I'm not ready to make any decisions."

"Then I'll make them for us." He smiled. "Deal?"

I laughed. "No deal."

He stuck out his lower lip in a pout as we twirled to a stop when the song ended. "Can we at least start seeing each other more often?"

"Oh, don't you worry." I took his arm as we walked back to our table. "I have a feeling you'll be seeing a lot more of me. A lot more."

He patted my hand. "Speaking as a reporter, may I say that that is the best news I've heard in a long time."

"And what are you two whispering about?" Maude teased as we sat down.

"Good news," I said. I winked at Ned, thinking how much fun Monday morning was going to be. "Very good news."

⚜ 15 ⚜

Stuck In Between

September 16, 1919

Dear Charlie,

*Thank you so very much for the card of
congratulations. I am keeping it on my desk. My first
days as cub reporter have flown by, absorbed as I
am by high-level preparations for President Wilson's
upcoming visit to promote the League of Nations. Just
for instance: I was assigned to pester City Hall for a copy
of the mayor's welcome speech, and to study railroad
maps to calculate the mileage our country's leader
has traveled in his campaign, and let's not forget the
two days spent attempting to find out whether Mrs.
Wilson prefers gardenias or violets. The jury's still out*

*on the latter topic, so our publisher, Mr. DeYoung, is
sending bouquets of each to the Presidential Suite at
the Fairmont. It is not all froth and foolishness. Mr.
Monson, the managing editor, has paired me up with
a more experienced reporter to cover some of the events
while the president is in town. That should be quite
thrilling.*

*How fascinating that Eddie Hubbard plans to
expand air service into Alaska. I am certain that the
far north is ripe for such an expansion. Do remember,
please, that there are polar bears and other unfriendly
creatures in such environs that might find a corn-fed
Iowa farm boy awfully tasty.*

*Yours truly,
Hattie*

I had decided not to tell Charlie that my newsroom partner
was Ned. Not when Charlie and I were back on "speaking"
terms, however fragile. I'd been an official employee of the
newsroom for seven days, and six of those had been spent in
Ned's company. After the first day or so, we found our way to
a good working routine, which mostly involved Ned telling
me what to do and my doing it. Everyone in the newsroom
was keyed up over the president's visit, working to find some
angle the *Call* or *Examiner* hadn't. When I had wondered
aloud about doing a piece on the female perspective on the
League of Nations, Ned had pooh-poohed it. "You've got
that working women's series already. You don't want to turn
into a one-issue reporter." I was generally grateful for Ned's

advice, but this hit me funny. We were too busy, though, to dwell on it much. We were all working long hours under tense conditions. It was not unlike trying to plant seed in a windstorm. At one point, I'd even seen Mr. Monson stick a cigar in his mouth—oblivious to the fact that he was already gnawing on one. I'd been dying to ask him about exactly when he planned to run my 49ers story, but the moment had not presented itself. Now we were all frenzied, what with the big day tomorrow. I glanced at the newsroom clock. Tomorrow would be arriving in just an hour.

"Two lunchtime speeches at the Palace Hotel and one at the Civic Auditorium in between." Ned shook his head as he read the schedule sent over to the paper by the president's secretary. "The man must be made of iron."

I thought of my own few train trips, wearying and gritty. Of course, the president traveled in a Pullman car, not in second class, like I had. But he was an old man, nearly sixty. I knew from my research that he'd be covering eight thousand miles in about three weeks, giving dozens of speeches, including those here in town. "He must really believe in the cause."

Ned didn't answer. He was already pounding away at his typewriter, lost in thought.

I picked an out-of-town newspaper off his desk. "President Goes to the People," it said. The writer was good. In a few paragraphs, he captured the gist of the story: that when the Senate refused to approve the creation of the League of Nations, President Wilson had gone straight to the people of America. He wouldn't take the Senate's no for an answer. The part I couldn't fathom was why senators would vote against the League if it was intended to help prevent future wars, as the president insisted. The whole affair must be more complicated than I realized.

"Is there anything else you need me to do?" I covered my mouth with my notebook to hide a yawn. "If not, I might head on home."

"What is this?" Miss D'Lacorte must have overheard me. "You want to sleep?" She shook her head. "This job has many rich rewards, including occasionally earning a living wage." She barked out a laugh. "But a full night's sleep? That's for copy readers, not reporters."

Blushing at my blunder, I looked again to Ned. "Anything I can do?" I guessed I could sleep when this was all over.

He stopped typing. "Confirm the parade route with the city desk and"—now *he* yawned—"scrounge me up some coffee."

The pot in the newsroom had gone dry, but I knew where to find some. And Bernice and Spot were more than happy to share. "Our Hattie, interviewing the president," Spot said with a shake of her head. "Makes me feel like I'm part of something awful special."

"I hate to break it to you, Spot, but I am only the errand girl. The closest I'll come to interviewing the president is typing whatever Ned writes up or Miss D'Lacorte calls in."

"Pshaw," said Bernice.

"You gotta think big, Hattie." Spot gave me a tap on the shoulder. "Big."

"Big." I filled Ned's coffee cup. "Got it."

Ned accepted the hot coffee gratefully. "Almost done here," he said. "You can decipher my handwriting." He handed me a couple of pages of his notes. "You type these pages and I'll type the rest. We'll be done in half the time, and then I'll drive you home."

I yawned again. "Deal." The faster I got home, the faster I'd be under my covers. The president's ferry was set to dock at nine-thirty in the morning, and we'd need to be in place hours before that.

Half an hour or so later, we were both finished. "Ready?" Ned asked.

I answered with a sleepy nod, gathered my things, and followed him to his car. The next thing I knew, Ned was nudging me awake. "Hattie, we're here. At the hotel."

"That's fine." I leaned my head against his shoulder. "Wake me when we get there."

"We are here, you goose. All ashore who's going ashore." He made a noise like a ferry boat whistle.

I sat up, rubbing my eyes. "Already?"

"And I'll be back again before you know it." He handed me my hat, which had somehow fallen into his lap.

I took it from him, and he slipped out from behind the steering wheel to open the passenger door for me.

He tugged me out of the car. "As much as I would love to take you home with me, I think you'd best get out."

That comment had better effect than ten cups of coffee. "Aye, aye, sir." I popped to my feet and saluted. "See you bright and early tomorrow." I remembered it was already to-morrow. "I mean, today."

Ned grabbed my saluting arm and tugged me to him, planting a kiss smack on my lips. "Good night, Hattie."

I pulled away, then brushed my lips. "Ned!"

He tugged me close again. "Yes, Hattie?"

I straightened my hat and smoothed my dress. "I'll see you in the morning."

I hurried inside and got ready for bed, but once I was under the covers, I felt as rattled as I had up in Eddie Hubbard's seaplane. Ned and I were like a team of oxen yoked to the same plow, and not simply because I was one of the few in the newsroom who could read his handwriting. He scarcely had to finish a question before I knew exactly what he wanted. I was great at research; he was great at putting all my research together. I was learning how to do that, too, but I wasn't in his league. Yet. I loved my crazy new job, despite the terrible hours. I wondered—would I have loved it as much without Ned? Was there more to our collaboration? And, more importantly, what did it mean that I had been tempted to kiss him back?

A few short hours later, I awoke to a party. A real hullabaloo! San Francisco had pulled out all the stops. Banners rippled above shop windows, flags flew on every corner, flower stands multiplied overnight. The street noise seemed jollier, and passersby moved on lighter feet. Cable cars and trolleys were jammed. As we passed in Ned's automobile, the men hanging off the sides of the trolleys waved and hollered. From the backseat, I hollered, too, caught up in the excitement. Flash rode in the front, snapping photo after photo.

Ned had paid one of his sources to meet us near the Ferry

Building to park the car. "Come back for us in an hour," Ned told him as he handed the man a few dollar bills.

"You got it!" A gold tooth glittered as he grinned.

We rushed into the terminal. There was no mistaking which ferry the president was riding—it was as splendidly adorned as the city itself and resembled a decorated birthday cake. All it lacked were candles on top.

"Excuse us, lady coming through." Part of Ned's plan was to use me much as Moses had used his staff to part the Red Sea. The gentlemen of the press, already snugged together like spoons in a drawer, at first responded to Ned's announcement out of instinct. Like that great sea, the multitudes parted, and we maneuvered our way to a choice spot closer to the front. Soon, the sager reporters refused to tumble to Ned's ploy, and we were stymied. Still, our vantage point was near enough to see the ferry dock and hear the band play a stirring Sousa march for the disembarking president and his first lady.

"Got enough?" Ned asked Flash, who nodded. "Then let's skedaddle and beat this mob to the next stop."

I'd nosed around and discovered that the president would ride up Market Street and then retire to the Fairmont Hotel to rest before his first speech. Ned dropped Flash and me off along the parade route and hurried back to the paper to file his initial report. A softer version of a battering ram, Flash pushed his way through the throngs, me tight to his side. As far as I could see, up the avenue and down, were people and people and even more people. All cheering at the top of their lungs. Soon the president's open car rolled into sight, escorted by the cavalry on their smartly prancing steeds, then marines, then sailors, all dashing in their crisp uniforms. Not far from us, a gaggle of schoolchildren waved flags and cheered, "Hip, hip, hooray!" Had I not been taking notes for Ned, I would have waved and cheered as well. There was something wonderfully infectious about it all.

"I've got enough photos," said Flash as the president's car drove out of view. He shouldered his gear bag. "Coming?"

I reluctantly tore myself away from the scene, showing him my notes. "I have to find a telephone and call this in." That was part of our plan, Ned's and mine: for me to be his eyes and legs. My next stop was the Fairmont. But that was our little secret. Ned's idea was that I would hang around the hotel and wait for a chance to catch the president on his own. The press all knew of his dislike for secret service men. Ned got the goods from a source in Seattle that the president snuck out there to the Pike Place Market to buy a bouquet of flowers for Mrs. Wilson. Ned was pretty sure he might get antsy again in San Francisco. And if he was, Ned wanted to be ready.

"All right. See you later, Hattie." Flash lumbered up the street under the weight of his equipment.

I hadn't told Ned, but I had decided his idea called for a bit of fine-tuning. And Florence was just the person to help me tune. She was more than happy to loan me a maid's uniform and to tell me which room was the Wilsons'. Less than an hour after arriving at the hotel, I had stashed my own things in a cleaning cart and was pushing it back and forth in the hallway, trying to look as if I belonged. I believe I was able to keep an outward appearance of calm, but inside, I was a mish-mash of misery. What if I was caught? My heart was pounding as loud as a parade drum. Nellie Bly had several times gone undercover in search of a story; how on earth had she done it?

"Miss?" a male voice behind me called out. "Oh, miss."

I turned, plastered on what I hoped looked like a maid's smile, and answered, "Yes, sir?"

"I seem to have locked myself out of my room. Just there." Dressed in the dark suit of a banker, he jingled the coins in his pocket. "Could you let me in?"

I stopped dead in my tracks. "Let you in?" The one part of the maid's disguise Florence could not provide was a set of master keys. I patted my pockets. "Oh, my. I seem to have left my keys downstairs."

"Well, go get them." He spoke like someone used to having others at his beck and call.

"Certainly, sir." I nodded and backed away toward the elevator. When the door opened, I stepped in, just behind a slim white-haired gentleman. That earned a frown from the elevator boy. "Service elevator," he hissed at me.

"Sorry. In a hurry." I smiled, hoping that answer would satisfy him.

"Lobby, please," the older gentleman asked.

"Yes, sir!" The operator answered with such enthusiasm I wondered if he was expecting a tip. I glanced at the older man. His skin was the color of Mr. Monson's cigar ash, and he leaned heavily against the brass hand railing that ran waist-high all around the car.

The boy pushed the button, but instead of smoothly descending, the car bucked and thumped and ground to a halt.

"Must have hit a bump in the road." The elevator boy smiled with his mouth, but his eyes didn't join in the joke. He pounded a few buttons. "We're stuck."

"Isn't there something you can do?" I asked, tongue clicking in my suddenly dry mouth. What if the cables gave way and we crashed to the bottom? What a wretched time to have a vivid imagination.

The old man cleared his throat. "Might you not call for help?"

I had been so wrapped up in my cloak-and-daggering that I had not really taken a good look at my fellow passenger. I leaned myself against the brass railing, too, as I realized who he was. The very man I'd been trying to corral!

"Oh, yes, sir!" The tassels on the elevator boy's shoulders swung as he reached for a red receiver. He turned a crank and shouted into the mouthpiece. "It's shaft number three. We're stuck." He listened intently, head bobbing up and down; then he disconnected. "They're working on it. Fast as they can."

"That's good news." President Wilson's smile softened his gaunt features. His eyes held a kindness that reminded me of Uncle Holt.

The elevator telephone shrilled. The boy answered it, listening intently. "Yes. I'll tell them." He set the receiver back in its cradle. "We're to sit tight. They should have us out of here lickety-split."

"Right, then," said the president. "I don't suppose either of you would care to share your thoughts about the League of Nations?"

One long hour later, we were released from our iron cage. Mr. Wilson—that was what he told the boy, Butch, and me to call him—was promptly whisked away by his aides. The hotel manager handed Butch and me bottles of icy-cold Coca-Cola. I rolled the contoured bottle against my sweaty neck and forehead, then sipped it gratefully. I decided that the manager didn't need to know I really wasn't in the hotel's employ as a maid. After the manager had gone back to his duties, I asked Butch if there was a telephone I might use. He took me to the bellhops' office.

I dialed and Miss D'Lacorte answered. I asked for Ned. "He's gone out," she said. "Is there something I can do?" I told her about what had happened. And she laughed. "Wait till Monson hears this. Don't go away." I heard the receiver being set down and then Mr. Monson picked up. "I have a story you might be interested in," I told him.

"What? How many balloons were sold along the parade route?" he asked. "Hattie, I'm busy. Big things happening. The president's speech is in less than an hour."

"Well, I've just been speaking with him for the past hour." I could feel a Cheshire cat grin spreading across my face. "But if you're not interested, I can always ring up the *Call*."

"Is this the gospel truth?" I could practically smell soggy bits of tobacco being spit into the telephone.

"Cross my heart and hope to die."

To me, he shouted, "Get back here! On the double." To someone on the other end, he shouted, "Stop the presses!"

Those words were even more delicious than that cold soda.

❧ 16 ❧

Byline Hattie Brooks

The President and
the Prairie Girl

An Unexpected Conversation

By HATTIE BROOKS

SAN FRANCISCO, SEPTEMBER 17: Little did I know that an elevator ride would lead to a thoughtful conversation with the great man who is leading our great nation into a new time. His beliefs are not always popular, but he defends his actions, saying, "The man who is swimming against the stream knows the strength of it."

Good and bad are often flip sides of the same coin. My first front-page article, with proper byline, elevated me from cub to reporter. The whole newsroom chipped in for a gardenia corsage, which I wore until it wilted. Gill let me know, however, that Ned hadn't chipped in for the flowers. I wasn't surprised. He was the senior reporter of our team, and I had ended up with the scoop. That wouldn't sit well with him. What was surprising was that Mr. Monson found me a Remington Junior typewriter—"Seventeen Pounds of Satisfaction"—with a complete set of working keys, and I began to find my name in his assignment book on a regular basis.

I sent clippings of my President Wilson interview to everyone—Uncle Holt, Perilee, Leafie, Rooster Jim, and Ruby. Even Charlie. He wrote right back, saying, "Nothing like starting at the top! Who's next? The king of England?" Good old Charlie, letting me know that he was on my side even if building up my dream meant tearing down part of his.

Ruby had telephoned—long-distance!—the very day her copy arrived. "I am certain I'll be home by the middle of October. We shall celebrate all of your accomplishments then," she'd promised. She had happy tidings, too. It turned out she'd lost her job not because of her absences, but because Mr. Wilkes had proposed! I was thrilled for her.

Any other time, I would have been so pleased about my change in circumstances, I could have smoked one of Mr. Monson's cigars myself. But my joy was tempered by tragedy. Only one week after my conversation with Mr. Wilson, he collapsed in Colorado and was rushed back to Washington, D.C. And one week after that, he suffered a stroke. Every day I checked the telegraph desk for the latest from the White

House about his health. Ominously, such reports were few and far between.

My new role was not all glamour. Most of my assignments were along the lines of the one Mr. Monson had given me yesterday, to write three hundred words on "Tulle: Fashion or Faux Pas?" And he had yet to give me a firm commitment on when he'd run my 49ers series. But today I had something meatier. I was typing up the last paragraphs when Mr. Monson stuck his head out of the office.

"Hattie, are you finished with that piece on the bus station kidnapping?" A thirteen-year-old girl had been found, dazed and tearful, at the bus station the day before. She claimed she'd been kidnapped, but her story didn't add up. Looked like an unhappy runaway to me.

I pointed to the page in my typewriter. "Nearly." I picked up the pace on my typing.

Mr. Monson came to read over my shoulder. "Who says it wasn't a kidnapping?"

"Well, from everything I heard, it sounded like she was making the whole thing up."

He chomped down on his cigar. "So now you're a detective as well as a reporter?"

"No . . ."

He yanked my story out of the typewriter, spinning the platen as he pulled. "This is not news. This is fantasy!" He tore the sheet into little bits and scattered them like snowflakes around my desk. "Call Detective West."

"I did. He hasn't called back yet."

He pressed his hand to his forehead. "You don't wait for

him to call you," he bellowed. "You call him. Again and again, if need be." He looked at the newsroom clock. "I'm closing the issue in thirty-five minutes and I want that story." He stomped back to his office.

I swept some of the paper bits into my hand and dumped them in the wastepaper basket. As I began to dial up Detective West, Miss D'Lacorte caught my eye. "You're lucky it was only your story he tore up. Sometimes he tears up the reporter!" Then she winked at me. "You're doing great, kid."

I made the deadline, turning in essentially the same copy I'd written before, because, as I'd suspected, the whole kidnapping story had indeed been a complete fabrication. The difference between the two versions, however, was the fact that in the second one, I had a credible authority, Detective West, confirming my hunch. I should have known better.

Ned breezed into the newsroom. "Hattie, how are things going?" His tone made me think we were on an even keel again. I started to tell him about my run-in with Mr. Monson, but he stopped me. "I've got lots to do here," he said. "Let's chat later. Over supper?" Flashing me a bright smile, he tossed his hat on the desk and pulled out the chair. "Be a pal and bring me a cup of coffee, will you?"

Miss D'Lacorte gave me a questioning look as I headed for the coffeepot. "Can I get you a cup, too?" I asked.

"My legs aren't broken," she answered. I knew what she was getting at, but I just laughed it off.

When I returned with the coffee, Ned was in conference with Mr. Monson. I set the cup on his desk. Of course, I couldn't help but read his notes as I did so. Because of his atrocious penmanship, Ned often left his notes lying around. I was the only one who could translate them.

And what I read rocked me back on my heels. I snatched up the papers and stormed across the room. "What is this?" My hands shook as I held out the sheets. "This is my story. *My* story."

"Now, now, Hattie." Mr. Monson tried to pat my arm.

"Ned?" I looked at my friend. Or at the person I had thought was my friend.

"Those were my notes," he blustered.

I wasn't about to stand down. "Those were my stories."

"Mr. DeYoung liked the idea of the Female 49ers but thought the stories needed a masculine slant. None of that sob-sister stuff." He shrugged. "What the publisher says goes."

I couldn't have been more stunned if Ned had slapped me. "I told those stories true." There was not one mawkish word in the entire series. Sob sister? Nothing could be further from the truth.

"The important thing is that those stories will reach thousands of readers," said Mr. Monson in a tone one might use when speaking to a child.

I thought of Tinny. And Florence. Yes, it was important that their stories were told. But it would never have occurred to the men standing in front of me to tell those stories if I hadn't given them the idea. "You talked to all of my sources? Even Tinny?"

Ned had the courtesy to look chagrined. "Well, yes. But I added a few others as well."

I shoved the papers at him. "That's big of you." There was nothing more to say. Ned had pitched me his own version of a snake ball, and I'd been struck out. I stumbled back to my desk and sat there, shaking with anger. And disappointment.

"It's business, Hattie." Ned edged over to my desk. "Nothing personal."

"What's going on?" Miss D'Lacorte stopped typing.

"It feels pretty personal." I bit the inside of my lip. Hard. If I cried now, I'd never forgive myself. I was no sob sister. I turned to Miss D'Lacorte. "Mr. DeYoung decided my 49ers series needed the male touch."

"What?" She pushed back from her desk. "I wonder how that happened." She glared at Ned.

"Let's step down the hall to talk." He tugged on my arm. "Out of this fishbowl."

"No." I hunkered down in my chair. "If it's business, we can talk here."

His face fell. "I don't want to compete with you."

"Then give me back my story."

"That's not my decision, it's Monson's, and it's been made."

At that, Miss D'Lacorte leapt up and dashed into Mr. Monson's office, shutting the door behind her. Hard.

Ned tugged on his tie. "I was hoping you'd go out to dinner with me. We'll paint the town red."

I stared at him. What on earth could he be thinking? "No, thank you." I pulled out a piece of paper and rolled it under the platen. I had no idea what I was going to type, but I needed to do something with my hands.

"Come on, Hattie. Don't hold a grudge." He made his puppy dog eyes at me. "Aren't you happy for your old chum?"

I counted to ten before attempting an answer. "I already have plans tonight." Plans that involved eating a tin of soup in my hotel room, but I wasn't going to tell him that.

"Another night, then," he said.

I started typing without responding.

He glanced over my shoulder. "What are you writing about?"

"Why do you ask?" I hit the carriage return. "Or did you plan on stealing this story, too?"

"Hattie!" Ned took a step back.

"I've got lots to do here," I told him, throwing his earlier words back at him. "Be a pal and get me a cup of coffee, will you?"

Ned stood there a moment and then walked away.

He never did bring me that cup of coffee.

❧ 17 ❧

Dinner and Disaster

October 12, 1919

Dear Hattie,

How's this for a headline: "Mechanic Moves North"? Maybe it's not as catchy as what you might write, but it tells the tale. There seemed no solid reason for me to refuse Mr. Hubbard's offer of a job in Alaska. And if anyone should understand about taking a chance to follow a dream, you should. I hope you will wish me well.

Yours truly,
Charlie

P.S. I promise to steer clear of polar bears.

There are earthquakes that shake the body, like the one I'd been through the month before. And then there are earthquakes that rattle the soul. Charlie's letter fell into that latter category. How could I say anything against his plans to go north, when he had not said a word against my plans to stay in San Francisco? And yet his letter left me as uneasy and uncertain as any seismic activity. As I made my way to work the day after receiving it, all I could do was wonder where my next shake-up would come from.

My solution to keep further disaster at bay was to put nose to grindstone. I cheerfully took whatever Mr. Monson assigned me, even the fashion bits. That strategy seemed to work, as several days went by without his making confetti of one of my stories. The gaps between my interactions with Ned stretched out too, until one Friday night, I saw him leaving with that sunny redheaded telephone operator I'd met my first day in the city. I experienced only the teeniest, tiniest twinge. The bigger twinge came when I learned that Ned was not only wooing someone else, but being wooed by the *Chicago Tribune*. I heard about it late one afternoon from Gill. Or rather, I overheard it. He threw a bone of encouragement to the pack of hopefuls ever waiting for their break. "Hold fast, you bright young men. Kirk may be leaving for another sheet. The *Chicago Tribune*."

"That so?" Ace joined the conversation.

Gill yanked a story from his typewriter. "Boy!" One of the office boys came running and took it to the copy reader. "He really got their attention with that idea for a series on women in the work world. Wouldn't be surprised if he's on his way up," he continued.

Ace cleared his throat and jerked his head my way.

"Oh, sorry, Hattie." Gill ran his hands through his hair. "I didn't think—"

I pasted a smile on my face. "Guess we'll have to take up a collection for him. Get him a nice going-away present."

"Yeah," Gill agreed halfheartedly. He glanced over at me. "Any ideas?"

"I know just what we could get him," Miss D'Lacorte called over.

"What?" Ace asked.

"A new knife." She pointed a red-painted fingernail at me. "He seems to have left his old one in Hattie's back."

Ace and Gill both chuckled and got back to work. Miss D'Lacorte plunked herself down on the corner of my desk.

"I will not beat around the bush." She rubbed the back of her neck. "You, my young friend, do not look happy."

"Of course I'm happy."

She pursed her lips. "Your fingers may be happy. Your hair may be happy. For all I know, even your knees are happy."

Her silliness got a smile out of me. "Sounds like I'm one big bucket of happiness."

"There's a hole in that bucket." She leaned in toward me. "The eyes."

I picked up a stack of papers on my desk, tap-tapping them into a squared-up sheaf. "I don't know what you're talking about."

"Neither do I, most of the time." She kicked off her pumps

and swung her legs as she sat, causing my already unstable desk to sway. "But one thing I do know: this job isn't everything."

"I know that," I said.

"Oh, really." Her legs stopped midswing, and she raised her left eyebrow. "Name one thing you've done for fun lately."

I continued cleaning off my desk. She didn't move from her perch.

"I went to the newsboys' picnic."

"That was work." She crossed her arms. "Not play. And whatever happened to that nice airplane mechanic?"

I leaned over to put the cover on my typewriter. A tear splashed on it.

Miss D'Lacorte slid off the desk and back into her shoes. "I need a steak and am tired of dining alone. We are going out to dinner." When she saw that I had my mouth open to protest, she held up her hand like a traffic cop. "Get your coat."

It was pointless to argue with Marjorie D'Lacorte. That much I'd learned since arriving at the *Chronicle*. I had to admit I would not mind skipping my usual tin of soup. "Dutch treat," I said.

"Your money's no good where we're going. So don't argue." She slipped into a navy flannel coat with a fur collar. "And tonight you call me Marjorie. Don't argue about that, either."

I didn't.

We walked through the crisp evening air, passing businessmen carrying briefcases and umbrellas, and ladies of the house with packages tumbling out of their arms. Soon we were in a part of the city that was new to me. Tall, narrow homes huddled together on the street like Aunt Ivy and her cronies at a coffee klatch. As we walked, I learned that Miss D'Lacorte—Marjorie—had an older brother, Tom, who'd been a pilot in the war. "When he turned up missing, I joined the Red Cross to find him. That's how I got in the reporting business. Sending dispatches home."

"So you found him?" I asked.

Her gloved hand rested in front of her mouth. "I did." After a moment, she continued. "Do you know what he'd done? Named his plane after me." She cleared her throat. I waited for more of the story but it didn't come.

Her pocketbook clicked open and she dabbed her eyes and nose with a handkerchief. "I've worked for lots of sheets. Chicago. Kansas City. Seattle, too. At the *Times*." She tucked her handkerchief away. "Now, there's an editor for you: C. B. Blethen. Cannot abide females in the newsroom."

"Even you?"

"Especially me." She gave a low chuckle. "Too bad I was their best reporter. Oh, did that give him conniptions." She took my arm, turning me to face the opposite side of the street. "Thar she blows." She pointed to a very elegant-looking restaurant.

We crossed over, stepped inside, and were quickly seated. I tried to stay upright when I read the menu prices. When the waiter came, I ordered a small salad and cup of soup.

"Oh, for crying out loud." Marjorie slapped her hand on the crisp white tablecloth. "Forget that nonsense. Bring us two steaks. With the works." The waiter seemed to know her, because very quickly a glass was set in front of her, two olives bobbing in a clear liquid. I was brought a ginger ale. Marjorie lifted her glass. "To you, Hattie." We clinked, then she sipped and sighed. "Ambrosia."

Dinner was delicious, but Marjorie's stories were even better. Some were hard to believe—could she really have danced with General Pershing?—but I didn't care. The evening was flying by delightfully, and without my once touching a can opener.

Dessert was apple pie. À la mode. I wouldn't need to eat for a week. "This is all so wonderful," I said. "Thank you."

She took one small taste of her pie, then slid the plate aside. "Your life is none of my business, of course. But let me offer some uninvited advice." She chuckled. "I suppose most advice falls in that category."

I swallowed and put my full attention on her. Advice from a seasoned reporter would be welcome, invited or not.

"This is a hard row you're hoeing, Hattie Brooks. I should know. I've been down it myself." She wet her finger to pick a crumb of crust off her dessert plate.

"I have to pay my dues. I know that." Though how many more column inches I could type about hemlines and hairstyles, I wasn't sure.

She studied me. "I'm not talking about the newspaper."

I frowned, puzzled. "I don't follow you."

"That's what I'm hoping."

It seemed as if she were speaking in code and I didn't have the key. "I'm sorry. I think I've missed something."

"I think you have, too." She leaned toward me. "I saw your face when you were with your mechanic at the airfield that day. Saw his, too." She whistled. "You seemed pretty glad to see him when you landed."

"We're good friends." The restaurant had grown stuffy. "We've known each other a long time."

"I could see that." Her eyes twinkled and I flushed. "You're pretty lucky to have a good friend like that. Not like some of the other men we know."

I studied my dessert plate, fully aware she was referring to Ned. "There's probably no one kinder than Charlie. But he wanted to make plans for *us*." I rested my chin on my hands. "And I need to make plans for *me*."

The waiter slipped the bill on the table. "And his plans and your plans don't mesh?" Marjorie asked.

"I can't get married!" I took a sip of ginger ale. "Besides, he's moving to Alaska."

She studied me. "That doesn't answer my question."

I couldn't believe it. Here I thought she had taken me out to dinner to give me a pep talk. "Miss—I mean, Marjorie. You know how hard it is in this business, especially if you're a woman. But a married woman?" I shook my head at the thought of that complication.

She glanced at the bill and opened her handbag. "If you are looking for someone to emulate, I am not that person."

Melted ice cream dribbled off my piece of pie onto the plate. I poked at it with my fork, but now had lost all taste for its sweetness.

She stood.

I could not forget my manners. "Thank you. It was delicious."

"You can find your way home from here?" she asked. "I'm around the corner."

No wonder the waiter had known what to bring her. "Yes, I'm fine." Well, I wasn't fine, but that was no call to be rude.

"Hazel Archibald," she said as we stepped outside.

"Pardon?"

"Hazel Archibald. Works at the *Seattle Times*. She's married." Marjorie finished buttoning her coat. "See you tomorrow."

I watched her walk away, reflecting on the evening. I now regretted the rich dinner sitting heavily in a stomach accustomed to one of Campbell's twenty-one varieties of canned soup. My heart was heavy, too. Why did Miss D'Lacorte have to bring up Charlie? It had taken all of my willpower to write back, and wish him well, after his letter. Why should it bother me that he was going after his dream? I'd expected him to allow me to go after mine.

And what of that dream? Sure, I had a job at the *Chronicle*. But I was no Nellie Bly, Grand Adventurer, Great Writer. Never would be. I was not even a Marjorie D'Lacorte. I was only Hattie.

I blinked back tears, longing for Ruby and her understanding heart. If only I could talk to her. She would help me figure out what to do. If only she weren't in Santa Clara . . .

Wait. Why couldn't I go to her? I began to walk faster. Ruby had been so kind to me; the very least I could do was spell her as she cared for Pearl. I had money saved up. Well, saved up for a trip north. But I wasn't sure I had the gumption for Seattle right now. I needed to feel useful, to think about someone besides myself. That was the ticket!

I knew I was on the right track with my thinking when I found the feather. A heavenly sign in answer to an unspoken prayer. And this was some feather, with its shiny coral shaft; it was that stunning color that had caught my eye. The pattern on the vane put me to mind of an appliquéd quilt block, as if an autumn oak leaf had pressed itself onto a shell pink feather. I picked it up, imagining the bird it had once adorned. It must be magnificent. Gill was a bit of a bird fancier; maybe he would be able to tell me about this feather. I slipped it into my pocketbook, feeling more chipper by the moment, even lighthearted enough to indulge in some window-shopping. I passed a milliner's and peeked in. Inside the hat shop, a woman was trying on an enormous hat. She was redheaded and petite, like Ruby. Very like Ruby.

The evening had definitely taken a toll on me. I rubbed my temple. Ruby was at her mother's, caring for Pearl. This must be wishful thinking on my part. Then my redhead stepped into better light and I came to a dead stop on the sidewalk.

This wasn't someone who simply looked like Ruby. It *was* Ruby! But that was impossible.

I could not breathe. Could not move.

The woman sashayed to the cash register to count out bills to pay the clerk. No doubt some of them from *my* cold cream jar. And there she was, pretty as pie, using them to buy a hat. An extremely ugly hat.

My dinner now threatened to spill itself over the sidewalk. I swallowed hard, stumbling blindly down the street. Ruby. Here. What did it mean?

It wasn't until I was back in my room, trembling on the bed that it hit me. The feather was not the sign I'd prayed for.

It was Ruby in that horrid hat.

18

The Stars Are in Alignment

Oh, what a tangled web we weave, when first we practice to deceive.   —*Sir Walter Scott*

I lay awake late into the night. Surely there was an explanation. Ruby had returned to town and hadn't yet had the opportunity to let me know. But what kept her from contacting me? I'd gone out for the evening, yes, but Raymond would've taken a message. Had there been a message.

As the sun slowly brought light into my room near dawn, it also brought light into my thinking. I had been overwrought from the evening. Marjorie's probing had upset me more than I'd realized. The rich food had thrown me off, too. And then there was the news about Ned. And Charlie. It was all too much. I wasn't thinking straight. How else to explain jumping to such a vile conclusion about Ruby? I would telephone her right away. And she would clear it all up. There'd be a good reason. A simple reason. Until my dying day, I must never let her know my hateful thoughts of the night before.

Deeply ashamed of myself, I somehow dressed and went downstairs. I double-checked with Raymond to see if there was a message for me. "Nothing," he said. "Not one thing." I glanced over the desk and saw that Raymond was drinking coffee. I believed him.

Gill greeted me when I arrived at the newsroom. "I know you're a big-time reporter now," he said. "But I spent an hour down in the dang-blasted morgue and couldn't find what I was looking for. Could you give me a hand?"

Anything to stall writing the article I'd been assigned: "What to Wear When You Motor." I nodded. "Sure, what do you need?"

He gave an uncomfortable laugh. "Now, don't think I'm another Ned," he said, "but your idea got me to thinking about women criminals." He made a face. "It's been a slow crime week."

He looked so pathetic, I had to laugh. "And that's a bad thing?"

"Very funny." He grimaced. "It is when you've got the police beat."

I picked up my notepad. "What are you looking for?"

"You ever heard of Mrs. Cassie Chadwick?"

I shook my head.

"There's a story for you! Happened in the late nineties.

She bilked a slew of bankers out of over four million dollars by claiming she was Andrew Carnegie's secret daughter."

"How?"

"Showed them a piece of paper with his signature, something like that. They thought she was worth billions, so they loaned her whatever she asked for." He shrugged. "The details are fuzzy now. But I don't want the piece to be about her. It needs to have a—"

"Local hook." I knew the drill. "Sure. I can poke around for you."

"I'd like to have three names—kind of a nice round number." He handed me a slip of paper. "Here are my notes so far."

I took it, glancing at the newsroom clock. "I can give you an hour," I said. "I have to finish my five hundred words on selecting one's wardrobe to match one's automobile." I tilted my nose up. "Very hoity-toity."

With a laugh, Gill said, "I'll take whatever time you can spare."

"I need to make a phone call first." I asked the operator to ring Ruby's apartment. No answer. Then I had her try Mr. Wilkes' office, too. Even though she was no longer employed there, they might know something. Mrs. Holm answered. "No, she's not here. I believe I heard Mr. Wilkes making arrangements to drive down to Santa Clara next weekend."

Oh, what a relief to hear such words! "If you do see her, would you please tell her I called?" Mrs. Holm said she'd be glad to. I nearly skipped to the elevator.

"Good morning, Miss Hattie." Leroy closed the elevator door. "Where you going?"

"The morgue, please." I held my notepad to my chest. A weight had been lifted, and I was ready to tackle whatever challenge Gill's query would provide.

When I pulled open the heavy wooden door, it felt like a homecoming. It'd been a while since I'd spent any time in this place. I stopped inside the door and listened for my voices from the past. I wondered what they were going to tell me today.

I decided to start with 1915. The exposition had brought thousands of people to town, and not all of them upright citizens. The number of articles about confidence men, check forgers, and insurance frauds was astonishing. And many of these "con men" were women! It didn't take me long to find some possibilities for Gill, including a Mrs. Denton, who claimed that her personal belongings—including all her jewelry and two sable coats—were in her automobile when it caught fire. Her mistake was in making that same claim five times, to five different insurance companies. There was a woman who professed to represent the British Patriotic Society of San Francisco and absconded with the money she'd raised to benefit "war sufferers." There were five stories about women who conveniently "forgot" they were already married and accepted the proposals of wealthy elderly men. And one about a church secretary arrested for juggling the church books. So much for the fairer sex being the purer sex. It appeared that women were equally capable of graft and greed.

It did not take me the hour to accumulate a sufficient number of notes for Gill. I certainly was glad to be done with this task. I felt I needed to go upstairs and wash my hands straightaway.

I was about to close the journal I'd been reading when a headline jumped out at me:

Victim Now Believes "Relative" Was Impostor; Complains to Police

How could a relative be an impostor? Apparently, a Mrs. Harriet Bliven, living with her five-year-old daughter, Gladys, had been visited by a woman claiming to be a cousin from the east. I read further:

> "She had a photograph of my mother," said Mrs. Bliven, explaining how she came to be taken in. But after the "cousin" helped herself to a few pieces of Mrs. Bliven's jewelry and $2,000 in cash that had been hidden in a desk, it became clear that there were no family ties. Police are looking for the cousin, who calls herself Rose Daniels, and a male accomplice. Police Lieutenant Richard M. Ingham reports that he has been contacted by the police department in Chicago regarding a similar case. The impostor there called herself Rose Danvers. She is described as being a well-dressed woman around 30 years old, about 110 pounds and five feet two inches in height, with a pale complexion and red hair.

I realized I'd been holding my breath. I let it out now, slowly. Shakily. I might question having seen Ruby the night before, but I couldn't question these words. Ruby had bamboozled Mrs. Bliven. Had she done the same to me? To Uncle Chester? Was she the friend he'd tried to cash the check for that time? Was she the reason he'd gone to Montana? There was only one person who could answer those questions for me.

Distraught, I hurried back to the newsroom and delivered my notes to Gill.

"You don't look well." He studied me. "Are you coming down with something?"

"Did you eat breakfast?" Marjorie asked, suddenly at my side.

Had I? I couldn't remember. Couldn't think. "I just need some fresh air."

"We'll cover for you." She reached over to a hook on the wall, pulled down my coat, and helped me into it as if I were a small child.

At first I didn't know quite where to go. But I found myself walking to the Pacific Building. To see for myself if Ruby was there. Mrs. Holm might be in on all this, too. I had no idea. The street was wrapped in the notorious San Francisco fog, making the few blocks' walk to Mr. Wilkes' office seem even longer.

As soon as I passed through that ornate portal, I sensed something was wrong. Mrs. Holm's always-tidy desk was covered in papers and files. Even with his office door closed, I could hear Mr. Wilkes talking. And he was not pleased.

"Oh, Hattie." Mrs. Holm glanced over her shoulder at the closed door behind her. "This is not a good time."

At that moment, Mr. Wilkes' office door opened and an egg-shaped little man walked out. Even without his summer boater, I recognized him. He'd been the one cornered by the astrology lady that day in the lobby of Ruby's apartment building.

"Thank you." Mr. Wilkes shook the man's hand. "I appreciate your help. And discretion."

"But of course. *Au revoir.*" The little man turned and acknowledged me with a tip of his hat. "You are Mademoiselle Brooks, are you not?"

I nodded and took a step back. "How did you know that?"

He cut a glance at Mr. Wilkes, who nodded. "Feel free to use that office," he said, pointing down the hall.

"Who are you?"

He presented me with his card:

LUCIEN K. GIGNAC, PRESIDENT
GIGNAC SECRET SERVICE BUREAU

"You're a detective."

He made an odd roll of his shoulders. "I prefer the term 'operative.' Come." He escorted me to the spare office, closing the door behind us. "Will that chair be comfortable for you?"

I decided to get right to it. "Why were you at Ruby's apartment that day?"

He had begun to seat himself and paused before lowering

his ample girth all the way down into the plush leather chair. "Perhaps you should tell me your story first."

I clutched my pocketbook even tighter. As I told him about seeing Ruby the night before, at the millinery shop, and the money I'd lent her, about the article I'd just found, and what I'd learned about Uncle Chester, he clucked his tongue, nodded his head, and steepled his fingers.

"Were they in it together?" I finished in a rush. Broken by the harsh truth I'd spoken, I could no longer hold back tears. "My uncle and Ruby, I mean."

He pursed his lips. "Things are not always as they appear."

"I'm not a child," I said. "I can handle the truth."

"Ah, but whose truth?"

I'd had enough of this double-talk. "What do you know about my uncle?"

He stroked his fastidious moustache. "Very little. He is deceased, is he not? And you are an—how do you say it?—an orphan."

That stopped me. "How do you know that?"

"It is my business." He waved his hands. "I have found out many things about you. I apologize. But it was important to know whether you were . . ." He paused. "Involved."

I nearly dropped my pocketbook. "Involved? In what?"

"I am not free to say. But, my dear mademoiselle, we are now very clear that you are innocent." His spectacles magnified the sadness in his eyes. "I regret I cannot tell you more. Now." He pulled a gold watch from his vest pocket. "I am very sorry, but I have a pressing engagement elsewhere."

I knew I was being dismissed. But I could not move from

the chair. It was as if my shoes were made of lead, not leather. "Is Ruby to be arrested?" I choked out the words. "What will happen to Pearl?"

Mr. Gignac's face scrunched into a frown.

"She's been ill." I leaned forward. "I gave Ruby money for the specialist."

"Mon Dieu." Mr. Gignac closed his eyes.

I couldn't breathe. Please, God, no bad news about Pearl. It would be too much to bear.

"I am so sorry, mademoiselle." He put his watch back in his pocket. "Pearl is yet one more of Madame Danvers' creations."

A window shade began to lower in my brain. "I feel faint. . . ."

He leapt up and came to my side, patting my hand. "Deep breaths, my dear. Deep breaths. This is a shock, I know."

"I don't understand."

His mouth formed a tight line. "There is no Pearl. Nor a grandmother in Santa Clara. It was a cruel hoax. . . ." His voice trailed off.

"How could she?"

"It is for the money." He sighed. "Always, for the money. Anything for the money."

I had confided my deepest grief to her, that I'd been unable to save Mattie. And she used it to manipulate me. "She's in town, isn't she? At the apartment." I pushed myself to stand. "I'm going to tell her what I think of her."

"I should not say this, but if you desire to have words with Madame Danvers, I would advise you to go now. Do not delay." He unfolded stiffly and moved away from me to stand upright again and opened the door. "Good day, Mademoiselle Brooks."

I didn't even bother to find a telephone to let anyone at the *Chronicle* know that I'd be out a while longer. Marjorie had said she'd cover for me, and I knew I could count on her. I raced to that familiar address on Union Street.

The old astrologer was in the lobby, petting her scroungy cat. "Ah, look, Figaro. It's our Scorpio friend," she said.

I brushed past her and ran to the elevator, mashing the up button. Hurry, hurry, hurry.

"No need to rush," the old lady said. "She's there."

The car arrived, and I pushed open the grate to step inside.

"All will be well, young lady," she called after me as I wrestled the gate closed. "For you, at least. Not for her." Her haunting laugh drifted up through the elevator shaft.

Ruby, or whoever she was, answered my knock. She nodded when she saw me there. "I thought that was you, last night." She stood in the doorway, not offering to let me in. "I can tell by your face that it was."

"We need to talk." I stepped forward.

"What's done is done." Ruby fiddled with the knob. "Let's not be tiresome."

"How about being honest?" I squeezed my way inside. "Tell me, Ruby, how's Pearl?"

She sighed and closed the door. "At least come in and sit down."

I didn't move. "Tell me."

"Oh, look!" She skimmed across the room to where a small stack of books rested on a chair. An open trunk sat on the floor beyond, partly filled with odds and ends.

"Are you leaving?"

"You must see what I've found." She snatched up the books and held them out. "You and Chester and your books. He couldn't bear to part with these. Me, I have no such sentiments about the things. Words, words, words. Who needs them? Give me a stack of Abe Lincolns any day. That's knowledge enough for me." She held the books out. "I want you to have them."

Something bitter rose up in me. "But don't you want to give them to Pearl?"

Her arms dropped, and she replaced the books on the chair. "You will think it a cruel trick of me, to play on your sympathy." Her voice was petulant. "But I was desperate."

"I told you about Mattie. That's why you invented Pearl." I felt woozy but was determined to stand on my own two feet. To face the full force of this ugly betrayal.

"Normally, I'd draw the line at conning someone your age, but you've been on your own some. You should be more careful." She beamed at me as if she'd done me an enormous favor. "You're angry at me now, but one day, you'll be grateful. I've taught you to be more cautious about trusting people." She turned away to continue packing.

"But why?"

She folded a paisley shawl and tucked it into the trunk. "You sound like Chester. He was so good at the con—what an actor!—but, oh, his silly little rules. We couldn't touch the clergy or farmers, or women with kids. Especially not women with kids. We would've been set for life if he hadn't gotten cold feet that time. All because the mark had a little girl. He wanted no part of it." She paused, then picked up that ruffled apricot dress to add to the trunk. "So I was going to turn him in. Otherwise, he'd ruin everything."

Her words turned me into a fence post; I could not move.

She flapped her hand. "Don't worry. He got wind of the whole thing. Fessed up himself, made bail, and skipped town." She smirked. "Went to Montana."

Was there no limit to this woman's heartlessness? Betraying my uncle then and me now? "How could you send that letter? The love token?"

She'd filled the trunk to the brim and was now struggling to lock it. "I thought maybe he'd come to his senses. Plus, I needed his help with . . . with something."

"Another Mrs. Bliven?"

Ruby managed to get the latches and pushed herself to her feet again. "I do wish we could chat longer, Hattie. But I'm in a bit of a rush."

I wanted to say something that would make a crack in Ruby's hardened, selfish heart. But to find such words would mean understanding how her mind worked, and I never wanted to lower myself to that. Never. I stormed across the room and grabbed Uncle Chester's books, somehow comforted by his refusal to cross a line.

"Good-bye, Hattie," she called after me, as cheerily as if she hadn't stolen my money and broken my heart.

I did not respond.

My hand trembled so that I missed the elevator button several times before connecting with it. I cradled Uncle Chester's books close on the ride down, rocking in place and praying for the strength to get back to my room at the hotel.

When the elevator door slid open, there was Mr. Gignac. I was not surprised to see him. I clutched the books closer to my chest. "These were my uncle's," I said.

"Of course." He held open the grated door so I could step out. "Madame is at home?"

I nodded. Then I noticed the two policemen in the lobby. My eyes snapped back to Mr. Gignac.

"I hope you have made your good-byes," he said. "Madame Danvers will be—how to say it?—unavailable for quite some time."

I made two telephone calls when I got back to the hotel. The first was to Gill; Ruby's story was going to be all over the papers sooner or later. He appreciated the tip. I also spoke to Marjorie and told her everything. "Take tomorrow off, kid," she advised. "We've got it covered here."

"I'll be in," I said. What good would it do to sit around and mope?

But mope was exactly what I did. All the rest of that awful day and into the night. I wallowed in misery on the bed, Uncle Chester's books scattered around me. Losing the homestead was one thing. That had been devastating, but not even the savviest farmer could survive a hailstorm at harvest. When I had surveyed the scene of my ruined crops—my ruined dreams—I'd thought I was seeing the worst I would ever see. But that was before Ruby Danvers.

She had said I would thank her someday for teaching me that life was about holding back, even holding back your own true self at times. In Ruby Danvers' dictionary, I was the prime example of a fool.

From my prone position on the bed, I could see my bouquet of feathers. The feathers I'd thought would symbolize my flight into a new life. Could I have been any more naive? Any more stupid? Hardly.

A thunderous clap of anger sounded inside me and I jumped out of bed, grabbed the feathers, ran to the window, and wrestled it open. "I hate you, Uncle Chester!" I screamed as loud as I could. "Thanks for nothing!" One by one, I let each feather in my collection drift from my hand out the window and to the street below to be trod upon by dozens of uncaring souls.

I threw myself back on the bed. So much for dreams. I had thought that learning about Uncle Chester would help me know myself somehow. All these months in the big city and I was no wiser than one of Rooster Jim's chickens.

In frustration, I shoved all of Uncle Chester's books to the floor, rolled onto my stomach, and pounded the mattress like a toddler throwing a tantrum. With a final punch to my pillow, I fell back, my left cheek resting on a cool spot on the sheet. In my direct line of sight, I saw the feather with the pink shaft. The one that led me to unravel Ruby's deception. On the floor, right next to the desk. It must've gotten blown back inside when I threw the other feathers out the window.

I pushed myself out of bed and snatched it up, ready to fling it outside, too.

Then something stopped me. A papery whisper like those I'd heard in the morgue all those times. Not words, but a sense of words: *She is wrong. She is wrong.*

She is wrong.

I did not believe in hocus-pocus, but every bit of me believed that Uncle Chester was trying to help me one last time. Trying to help me see that Ruby had it crossways. I brushed that feather against my hot cheek.

If trusting others was foolish, well, much better to be a fool. If you didn't trust, didn't open your heart up to people, to one special person, that was what made you a failure. Not a summer hailstorm. Not a homestead left behind. Not a huckster in the form of a false friend.

I curled up on the chair by the window, looking out at the stars blinking bright and brave, absorbing their light and promise. Then I crawled into bed and said my prayers, closing with, "And God bless Uncle Chester. Amen."

❧ 19 ❧

Taking Pen in Hand

" 'Of course, she didn't seem like a criminal,' explained
Lucien Gignac. 'That's because she was very good at
what she did.' "
>   —*from* Inside the Female Criminal Mind,
>   *by Gill Short*

It turned out that despite neither of us having ever seen her,
Mr. Wilkes and I had both been contributing to the imagi-
nary Pearl's health improvement fund; he, understandably, at
a much higher rate than I. When he learned of my situation,
he telephoned to offer to replenish my Pond's Cold Cream jar,
but as it had been drained through no fault of his, I couldn't
accept that kind offer. I did, however, accept an invitation to
be his guest when the great reporter Ida Tarbell spoke to the

San Francisco Club. To my mind, that was the better part of the bargain. Miss Tarbell's closing words, "Imagination is the only key to the future. Without it none exists—with it all things are possible," not only thrilled me, they propelled me to action.

Miss D'Lacorte proved to be a trusty confidante when I approached her the morning after Miss Tarbell's speech. I showed her the letter I'd composed, and she approved. "Looks like you'll need a recommendation from me to C. B. Blethen," she said.

"You don't know what the answer will be," I pointed out.

"Oh, there can only be one answer to correspondence like that." She hit the carriage return on her typewriter with a flourish. "If you don't get a yes, I'll eat Gill's ridiculous new tie." We both grinned at Gill's bemused expression.

With that vote of confidence, I sealed up the envelope containing one concise letter and one delicate object, pasted on a stamp, and headed to the post office, dodging Mr. Monson, who was no doubt bearing down on me with another gloves-and-gown assignment. "I'll be back in a jiff," I told him. His response was to chomp harder on that ever-present cigar.

I had my reply in less than two weeks. With trembling hands, I opened it and began to read.

October 23, 1919

Dear Hattie,

I am in receipt of your letter, and the colorful feather tucked inside, though am perplexed about its

*significance. As for the letter itself, it seems that the
women's suffrage cause has done more than bestow upon
the weaker sex the right to vote. Apparently, it now gives
women the right to make proposals of marriage. What
next? I shudder to think. It is a thoroughly disturbing
chain of events.*

*I am sorry, but there is only one action I can take.
And that is to paste said letter into a scrapbook. That
way, I will have proof for our grandchildren that their
grandmother was always a brazen woman.*

*As for your worries about not setting a date too soon: I
have loved you since I was fifteen and don't see that state
of affairs changing, whether there is a ring on your finger
or not.*

*Yours. Always.
Charlie*

*P.S. Mr. Boeing was pleased to learn I would be staying
in Seattle.*

❧ 20 ❧

Till Niagara Falls

September 6, 1923

Dear Perilee,

I felt as fetching as a magazine model in the traveling suit you made me. Charlie said I was the prettiest girl on the train. But isn't that what any new husband would say? And wasn't it sweet of Mr. Blethen to see his ace reporter off on her honeymoon?

I don't know what will be the bigger adventure: this cross-country trip or making a home with Charlie in Seattle. Home. Simply writing this word makes me feel like I'm blanketed, safe and warm, under one of your quilts. As big as I dreamed on the Montana prairie, I never dreamed that Miss Hattie Here-and-There would ever find such a home, and one so solidly built, not only with planks and stone, but with the hearts of those who love her. It's been quite the journey from orphan homesteader to married reporter, and I could not have managed without help from so many, including one scoundrel uncle and a strudel-baking friend. You know it galls me to do so, but I am compelled to agree with Aunt Ivy on this point: the Lord does work in the most mysterious ways.

I must stop now. We are getting out to stretch our legs at Glacier Park, and I want to pop this in the mail.

Yours till Niagara Falls!
Hattie Inez Brooks Hawley

Acknowledgments

Mine might be the only name on the front cover, but I depend on the kindness of strangers to make a book like this happen, including aviation buffs Roger Cain, Howard "Ace" Campbell, and Bill Larkins; David Coscia, archive director, Southern Pacific Historical & Technical Society; Paula Becker, staff historian, and all the amazing history hot shots at historylink. org, who keep Washington state's past alive and lively; Sharon Levin, who polled her writer/historian friends for an idea for a San Francisco scandal circa 1915; Ellen Keremitsis, reference staff, North Baker Research Library, California Historical Society; Mimi MacLeod and Bob Maxwell, who helped me understand those fire-breathing dragons called linotype machines; and Bill Sornsin at the Great Northern Railway Historical Society, for train schedules and routes. Tami J. Suzuki, librarian at the Daniel E. Koshland San Francisco History Center of the

San Francisco Public Library, introduced me to *San Francisco Chronicle* librarian Bill Van Niekerken, who pointed me toward the invaluable *Journalism in California* by John P. Young; Tom Carey, at the San Francisco History Center, helped verify that the Hyde Street cable car on this book's cover would indeed have been running during Hattie's time in the City by the Bay; Thom Hindle, camera historian, gave me the brand name of Flash Finnegan's camera; and the very efficient, knowledgeable, and generous Lew Baer, editor of the San Francisco Bay Area Post Card Club, authenticated dates of the cards included in this book. The postcard in Chapter 10 appears courtesy of Lew from his private collection. I am also grateful to every research librarian who cheerfully answered my crazy and never-ending questions. Blessings on you all for extending a hand to a writer in need.

Profound thanks to my editor, Michelle Poploff, for saving me from countless literary embarrassments, and to her assistant, Rebecca Short, both of whom believed I could actually finish this book (though some months later than promised), and my agent, Jill Grinberg, who is a whole lot of fun in addition to being one very sharp cookie. I owe a glass of wine to Karen Cushman and Barbara O'Connor (my "old broads who don't do vampires" buds) and Jenni Holm and Cynthia Lord, all of whom comforted, commiserated, and occasionally cajoled each time I hit the wall. Nothing I write happens without Mary Nethery, who never wearies of reminding me that plot is always a good addition to any novel. My husband, Neil, and Winston the Wonder Dog spent many hours listening to me talk out this story on our daily walks. Neil: for a CPA, you really know how to think outside the boxes.

This book would not exist without the women who made headlines, like Nellie Bly and Ida Tarbell, and the women who deserved to, including some of my relations. The more I read, the more I realize our foremothers kicked butt, and it's a crying shame that too few of their stories are out there.

Author's Note

When I left Hattie at the end of *Hattie Big Sky*, I had no intention of writing another book about her. But so many readers have emailed or written to find out what happened next—I was even once collared in the grocery store!—that I began to wonder about it myself.

I initially envisioned Hattie taking a road trip, a concept inspired by the delightful book *Eight Women, Two Model Ts, and the American West* by Joanne Wilke. Trust me, I tried to send Hattie on the road, but she dug in her heels. It turns out that all of those Honyocker's Homilies gave her the writing bug, big-time. She wanted to be a reporter and needed to get to a newspaper, not behind the wheel of a Model T.

When I taught writing, I used to promise my students that their first draft would contain everything they needed to complete a story. Though it is certainly not a first draft, rereading

Hattie Big Sky brought that home to me in the guise of an uncle who'd called himself a scoundrel. Many books start with a writer asking "What if?" So I asked myself, "What if Hattie set out to solve the mystery of Uncle Chester's life?" He'd gone to Montana from somewhere else, but where? When I realized he could have been in San Francisco around the time of the 1915 Panama Pacific International Exposition, I knew that was where Hattie was going to end up. A chance encounter with an article about love tokens fashioned from old coins (learn more at lovetokensociety.org) paved the way for Ruby Danvers and a delicious dilemma for Hattie.

Being the prima donna that she is, "Empress of Emotion" Vera Clare swept to the center stage of this novel early on. She initially garnered a starring role, and is not pleased that most of her story ended up in a computer file labeled "deleted scenes." Though vaudeville was waning by the 1920s (it couldn't compete with films), that traveling troupe lifestyle seemed the perfect vehicle for transporting Hattie from Montana to California. Issues of *Theater* magazine from 1919 educated me about Hamlet traps, second boys, and other theater lore and terms.

Historic San Francisco came alive for me through three resources: my treasured copy of the 1921 edition of *The New World Atlas and Gazetteer,* published by P. F. Colliers and Sons, *Women and the Everyday City: Public Space in San Francisco, 1890–1915* by Jessica Ellen Sewell, and the 1919 Crocker-Langley San Francisco directory, which is where I found the listings for the Hotel Cortez, Clinton's Cafeteria, and Praeger's department store. These books helped me confidently move Hattie around town. Places like the Fairmont Hotel and Lotta's Fountain still exist; you can visit them yourself. The Chronicle

Building is privately owned but still standing and ready for a photo op. And that famous Golden Gate Bridge? Hattie never saw it. (In Chapter 11, Hattie flies over the Golden Gate *channel*.) Construction on the bridge didn't begin until 1933, fourteen years after she lived in San Francisco.

If you wonder what life was like for early women reporters, do read *Bylines: A Photobiography of Nellie Bly* by Sue Macy and *Ida Tarbell: Pioneer Investigative Reporter* by Barbara A. Sommervill. To further satisfy your craving for newsprint, check your local library's online database to see if you can access the historic *New York Times*. Besides learning the news and opinions of a particular time period, you can also sleuth out business names and locations, as well as prices of food and clothing. The *Times* is where I found out that Campbell's made twenty-one varieties of soup in 1919, each selling for twelve cents a can. And the room in which Hattie heated all those cans of soup on a hot plate would have cost $2.50 a week, a detail I uncovered by reading old classified ads in the *San Francisco Chronicle*— the same paper Hattie worked for. Warning: Reading old newspapers is addictive!

One of the things that struck me as I read the newspapers from 1915 to 1920 was the number of reports of people taking advantage of others. This time period is sometimes called the Golden Age of the Con, and now I know why. Whether it was a crooked card game, a scam to sell fake souvenirs from the Panama Pacific International Exposition, or a bad check, there was at least one reference to crime and corruption in every issue I read. In some ways, that more innocent age made it easier for crooks. Information traveled slowly, and this was well before the days of any CSI units. In addition, banking practices like making blank counter checks available to department stores (see Chapter 5) provided opportunity to cheaters who merely had to write fake account numbers on those counter checks. There really was a Cassie Chadwick, whom I encountered in *The Incredible Mrs. Chadwick: The Most Notorious Woman of Her Age* by John S. Crosbie, and she is the inspiration for Ruby Danvers. The con Ruby tried to pull on Mrs. Bliven is based on one I read about in the pages of the *Chronicle*.

If you haven't figured it out yet, I am a compulsive researcher, working hard to bring the past alive accurately. (That doesn't mean I don't make mistakes; I ask forgiveness in advance for any glitches you discover.) Favorite investigative techniques include studying old newspapers and atlases, and reading personal journals and accounts. I even browse eBay for photos, letters, and postcards—anything to help me understand a particular era. Like Hattie, I have been known to disappear in dusty archives and newspaper morgues. But this book in your hands is a work of historical *fiction*. In order to give Hattie a compelling story to wander around in, I did juggle some facts.

For example, to my knowledge, the pilot Eddie Hubbard never gave flying demonstrations in San Francisco. Nor does it appear that there were any civilian seaplanes taking off from the Presidio's Flying Field during Hattie's time there. But the opera great Luisa Tetrazzini did indeed hire Eddie to give her a flight-seeing tour of the city of Seattle. As described in *Hattie Ever After,* the cool air was deemed harmful to the Florentine Nightingale's voice, so a woman reporter, Hazel Archibald (writing as Dora Dean), took her place in the passenger compartment of Eddie's seaplane. The lead of Hattie's article about her adventure is taken directly from Dora/Hazel's own words in the *Seattle Times* on January 2, 1920.

President Wilson did undertake a grueling tour around the country to win popular support for the League of Nations, a course of action that exacted a huge physical toll. He collapsed in Pueblo, Colorado, on September 25, 1919, and on October 2 he suffered a terrible stroke. There is no record of his getting stuck in an elevator during his San Francisco stop (he actually stayed at the St. Francis, not the Fairmont). That incident was fabricated to give Hattie a juicy scoop.

It is unlikely that Hattie would have been able to repay Uncle Chester's four-hundred-dollar IOU as quickly as she did. In 1920, a professional baseball player earned about five thousand dollars a year. The average male office worker's annual income was about twelve hundred dollars; female office workers made considerably less, around eight or nine hundred. For the sake of the story, I beefed up Hattie's earning power to pay off the debt sooner.

One of the reasons I am drawn to writing historical fiction is that it can help us understand ourselves in the here and now. To be fair, I should say it helps me understand *myself* in the here and now. It may do the same for you. Young women had limited options in the early nineteen hundreds, yet girls like Hattie not only survived, they thrived. Elizabeth Jane Cochran, better known as Nellie Bly, was only eighteen when she took on her first reporting assignment. And for every Nellie Bly who achieved fame and fortune, there were hundreds of plucky unknowns whose stories are equally fascinating. Take Hazel Lagenour, for example, who was the first woman to swim across the Golden Gate channel—a formidable challenge. She did it on August 19, 1911. You can watch a silent movie of the event at archive.org/details/ssfGGSWIM. The very next day, August 20, Nellie Schmidt beat Hazel's time, swimming the channel in forty-two minutes. Though men had swum that waterway before, none of the men who attempted to swim across that August day with Nellie succeeded. I have to cheer when "ordinary" females like Hazel and Nellie do something extraordinary. I am fortunate that my work allows me to poke around in the past, uncovering amazing and inspiring anecdotes of strong girls and women, so that I can bring them to my readers' attention.

Yes, I did a copious amount of research for this book. But my efforts were fueled by the desire to get *this* story—the story of seventeen-year-old orphan Hattie Inez Brooks trying to find her place in the world—absolutely right. Feel free to let me know how I did in that regard.

About the Author

A snippet of a family story transformed Kirby Larson from history-phobe to history fanatic and led her to write the Newbery Honor–winning novel *Hattie Big Sky*. She now loves nothing better than peering at microfiche, rummaging in archives, and rescuing old letters and postcards in her efforts to poke around in the past. Her most recent book is *The Friendship Doll*.

A *New York Times* bestselling author, Kirby has partnered with her dear friend Mary Nethery to write award-winning nonfiction picture books, including *Two Bobbies: A True Story of Hurricane Katrina, Friendship, and Survival*.

When Kirby is not digging around in history, she is walking on the beach with her husband, Neil, and Winston the Wonder Dog. She loves looking for sea glass, wishing rocks, and pieces of history others pass right on by. Learn more about her at kirbylarson.com, or read her blog at kirbyslane.blogspot.com.